Teddy Scares®

 Published by Ape Entertainment, PO Box 7100, San Diego, CA (www.ApeComics.com). Printed in Hong Kong.

ape entertainment

Applehead factory

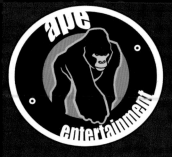

APE ENTERTAINMENT

Brent E. Erwin
Co-Publisher / General Partner
BErwin@Ape-Entertainment.com

David Hedgecock
Co-Publisher / General Partner
DHedgecock@Ape-Entertainment.com

Kevin Freeman
Managing Editor
KFreeman@Ape-Entertainment.com

Drew Rausch
Art Director
DRausch@Ape-Entertainment.com

Michael Murphey
Marketing Coordinator
MMurphey@Ape-Entertainment.com

Company Information:
Ape Entertainment
P.O. Box 7100
San Diego, CA 92167
www.ApeComics.com

For Licensing / Media rights contact:
William Morris Agency, LLC
Scott L. Agostoni
SLA@wma.com

For Advertising information contact:
Brent E. Erwin
BErwin@Ape-Entertainment.com

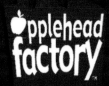

FOR APPLEHEAD FACTORY, INC.
TEDDY SCARES BASED ON
THE CHARACTERS CREATED BY:
JOE DIDOMENICO & PHIL NANNAY.

TEDDY SCARES®

STORIES WRITTTEN BY: JIM HANKINS

LETTERING BY:
DAVID HEDGECOCK

PIN-UPS BY:
DREW RAUSCH, ROB GUILLORY, AND SAM HEIMER

REGULAR COVER BY:
BEN ROMAN & JORGE MOLINA

ALTERNATE COVER BY:
CHRIS MORENO

BACK COVER BY:
CHRISTINE LARSEN

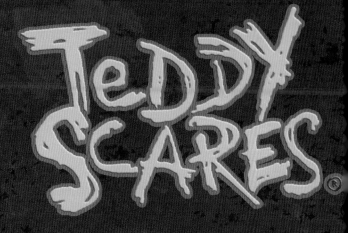

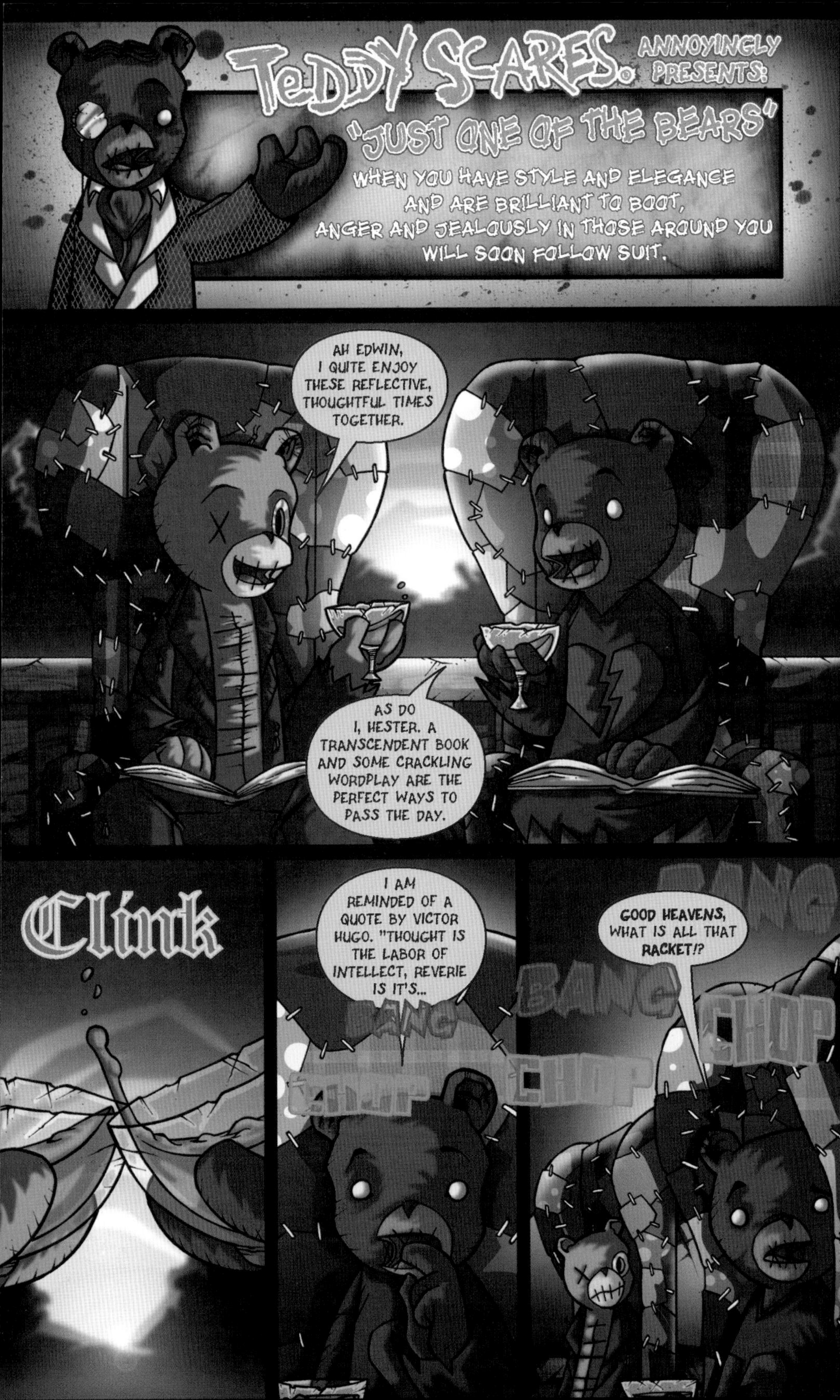
TEDDY SCARES. ANNOYINGLY PRESENTS:
"JUST ONE OF THE BEARS"
WHEN YOU HAVE STYLE AND ELEGANCE AND ARE BRILLIANT TO BOOT, ANGER AND JEALOUSLY IN THOSE AROUND YOU WILL SOON FOLLOW SUIT.
AH EDWIN, I QUITE ENJOY THESE REFLECTIVE, THOUGHTFUL TIMES TOGETHER.
AS DO I, HESTER. A TRANSCENDENT BOOK AND SOME CRACKLING WORDPLAY ARE THE PERFECT WAYS TO PASS THE DAY.
Clink
I AM REMINDED OF A QUOTE BY VICTOR HUGO. "THOUGHT IS THE LABOR OF INTELLECT, REVERIE IS IT'S...
BANG
BANG
CHOP
CHOP
GOOD HEAVENS, WHAT IS ALL THAT RACKET!?
BANG
CHOP

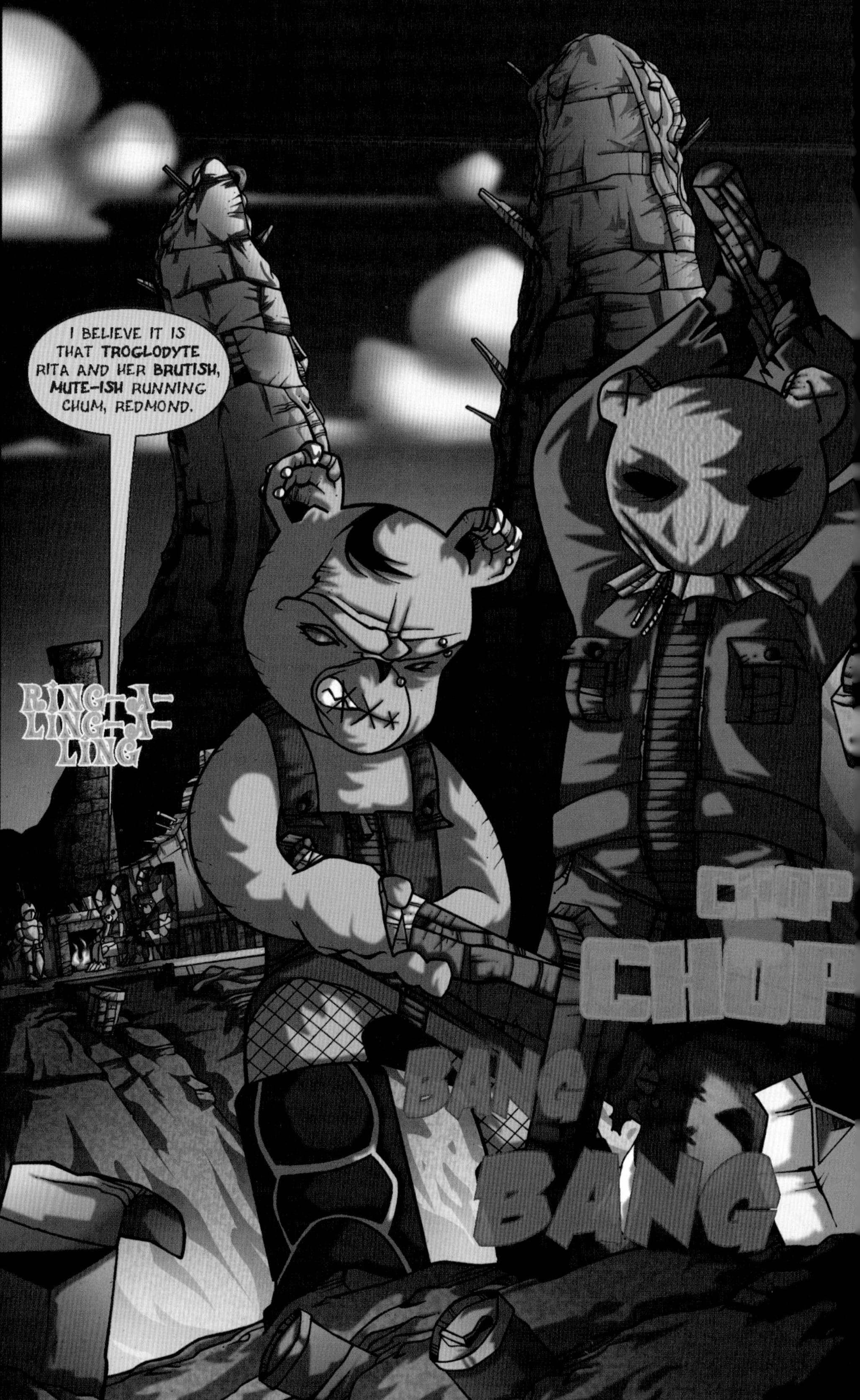
I BELIEVE IT IS THAT TROGLODYTE RITA AND HER BRUTISH, MUTE-ISH RUNNING CHUM, REDMOND.
RING-A-LING-A-LING
CHOP
CHOP
BANG
BANG

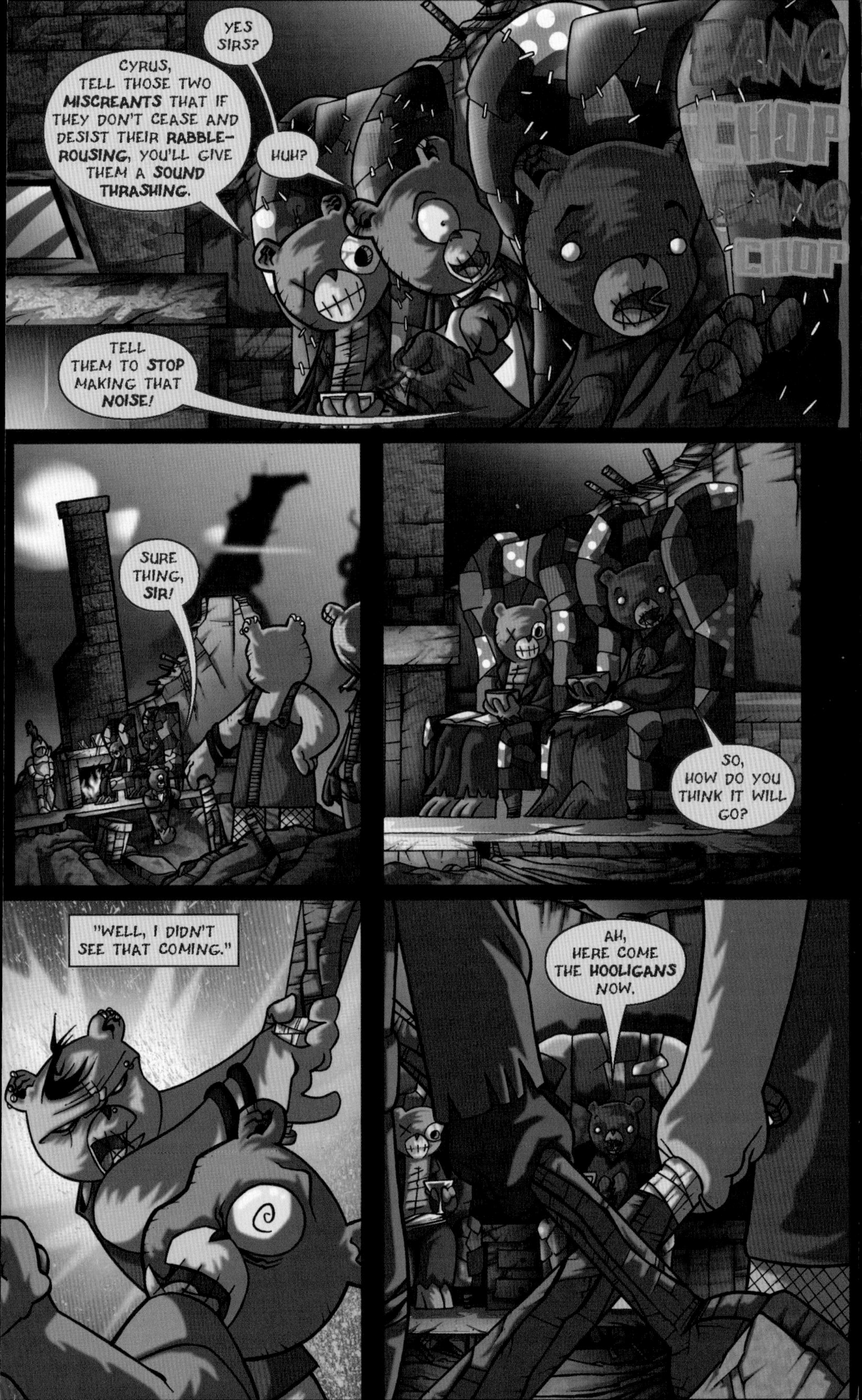

CYRUS, TELL THOSE TWO **MISCREANTS** THAT IF THEY DON'T CEASE AND DESIST THEIR **RABBLE-ROUSING**, YOU'LL GIVE THEM A **SOUND THRASHING**.
YES SIRS?
HUH?
BANG
CHOP
BANG
CHOP
TELL THEM TO **STOP** MAKING THAT **NOISE**!
SURE THING, **SIR**!
SO, HOW DO YOU THINK IT WILL GO?
"WELL, I DIDN'T SEE THAT COMING."
AH, HERE COME THE **HOOLIGANS** NOW.

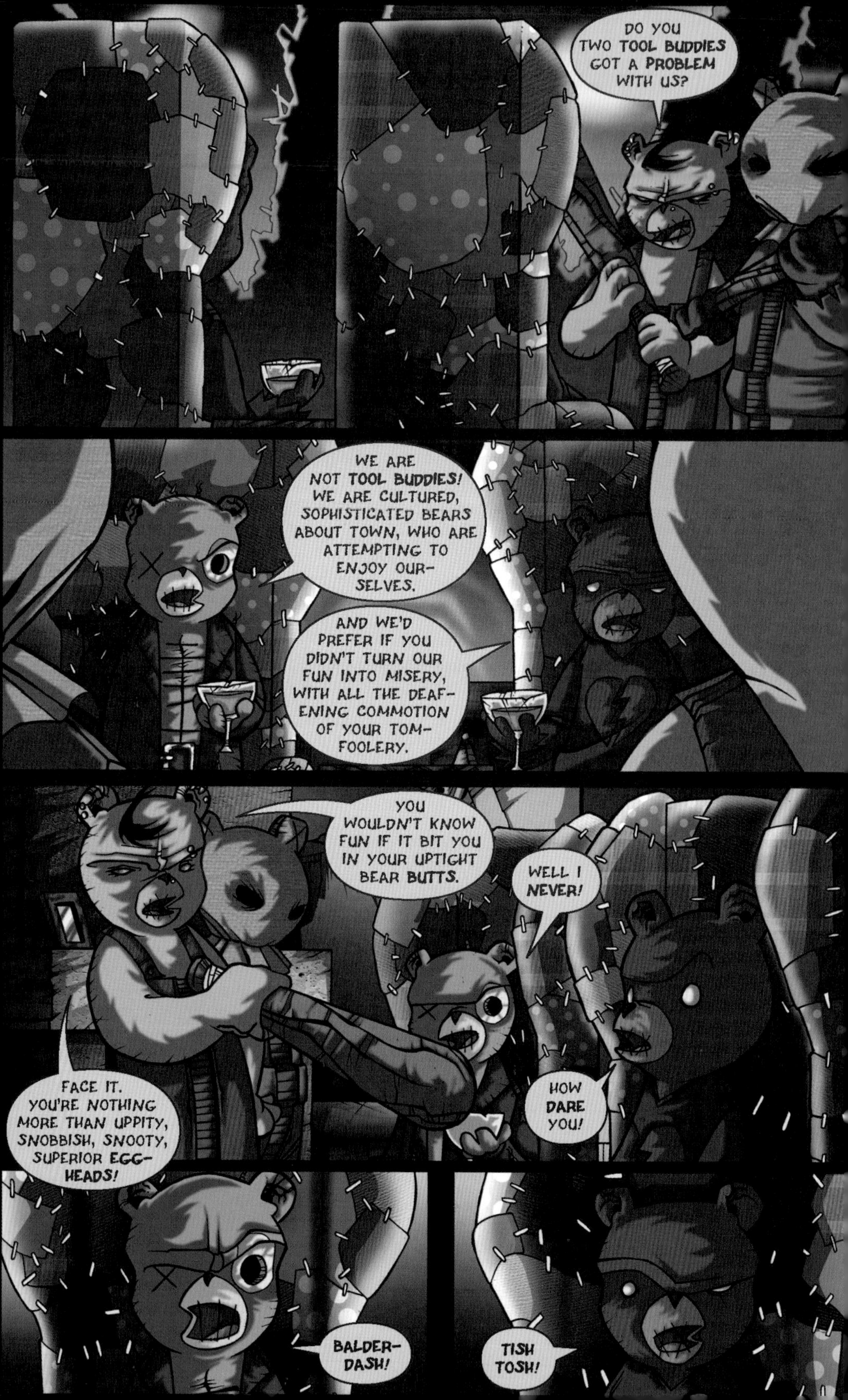
DO YOU TWO TOOL BUDDIES GOT A PROBLEM WITH US?
WE ARE NOT TOOL BUDDIES! WE ARE CULTURED, SOPHISTICATED BEARS ABOUT TOWN, WHO ARE ATTEMPTING TO ENJOY OUR-SELVES.
AND WE'D PREFER IF YOU DIDN'T TURN OUR FUN INTO MISERY, WITH ALL THE DEAF-ENING COMMOTION OF YOUR TOM-FOOLERY.
YOU WOULDN'T KNOW FUN IF IT BIT YOU IN YOUR UPTIGHT BEAR BUTTS.
WELL I NEVER!
FACE IT. YOU'RE NOTHING MORE THAN UPPITY, SNOBBISH, SNOOTY, SUPERIOR EGG-HEADS!
HOW DARE YOU!
BALDER-DASH!
TISH TOSH!

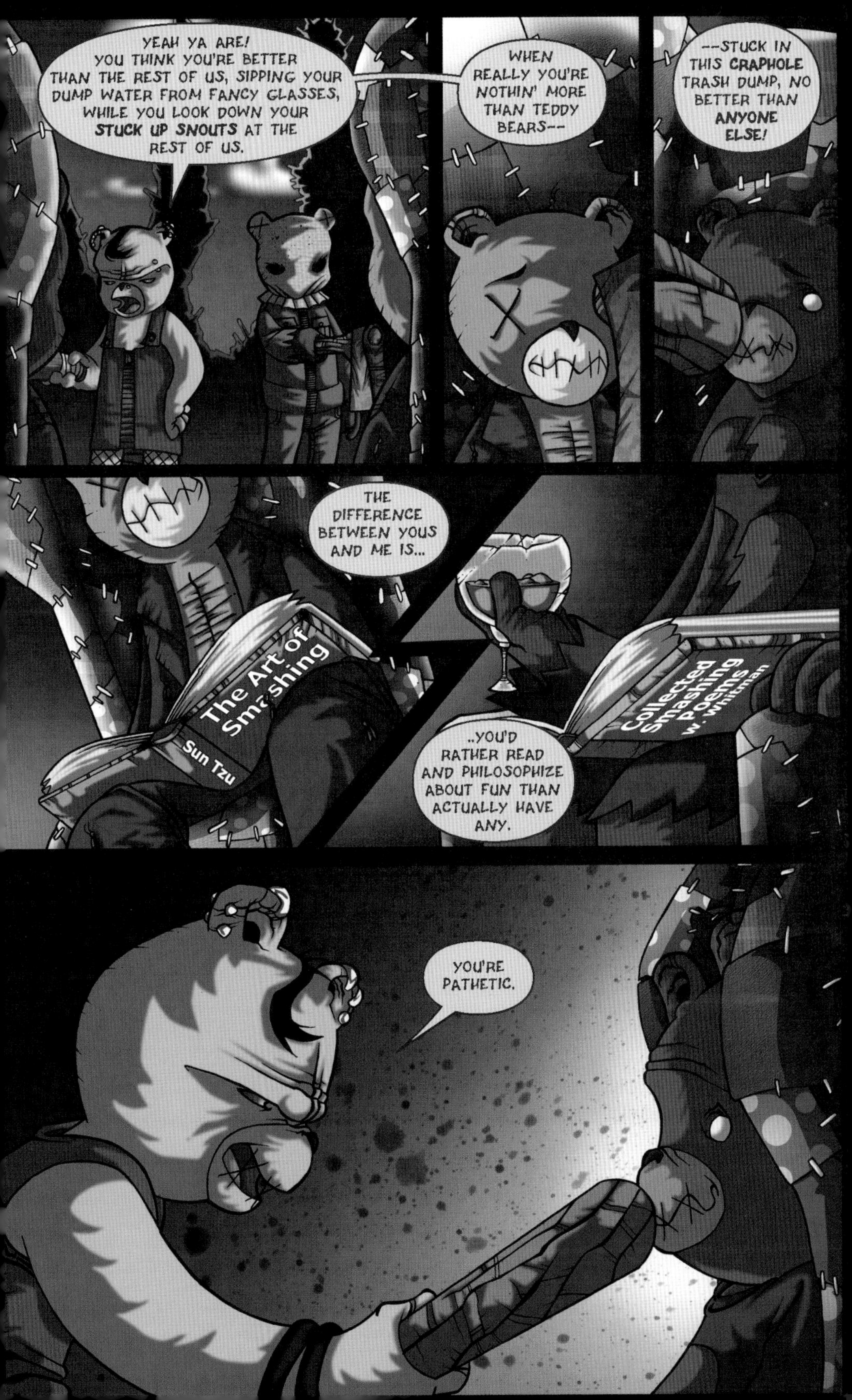
YEAH YA ARE! YOU THINK YOU'RE BETTER THAN THE REST OF US, SIPPING YOUR DUMP WATER FROM FANCY GLASSES, WHILE YOU LOOK DOWN YOUR **STUCK UP SNOUTS** AT THE REST OF US.
WHEN REALLY YOU'RE NOTHIN' MORE THAN TEDDY BEARS--
--STUCK IN THIS **CRAPHOLE** TRASH DUMP, NO BETTER THAN **ANYONE** ELSE!
THE DIFFERENCE BETWEEN YOUS AND ME IS...
The Art of Smashing
Sun Tzu
Collected Smashing Poems
W. Whitman
..YOU'D RATHER READ AND PHILOSOPHIZE ABOUT FUN THAN ACTUALLY HAVE ANY.
YOU'RE PATHETIC.

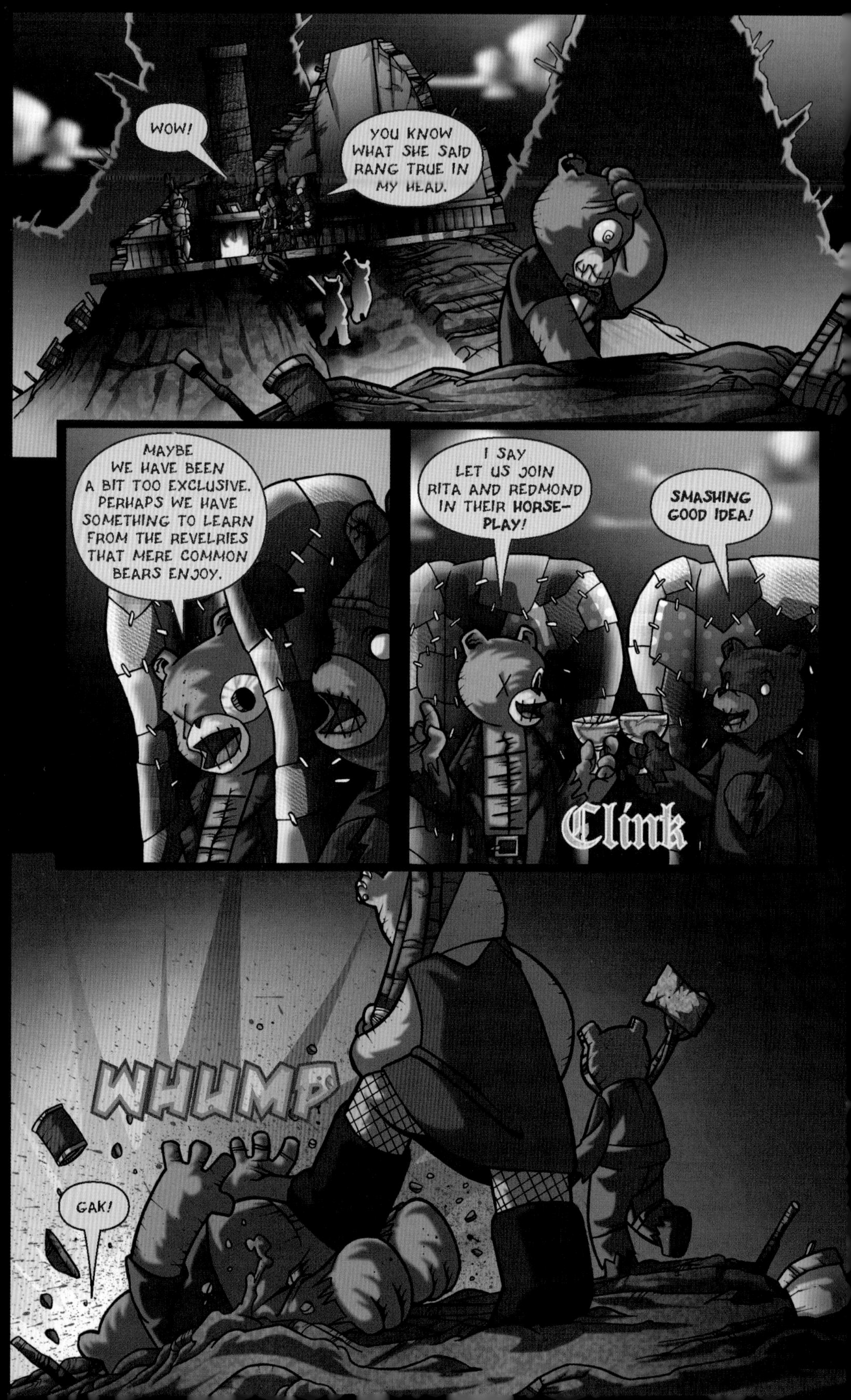
WOW!
YOU KNOW WHAT SHE SAID RANG TRUE IN MY HEAD.
MAYBE WE HAVE BEEN A BIT TOO EXCLUSIVE. PERHAPS WE HAVE SOMETHING TO LEARN FROM THE REVELRIES THAT MERE COMMON BEARS ENJOY.
I SAY LET US JOIN RITA AND REDMOND IN THEIR HORSE-PLAY!
SMASHING GOOD IDEA!
Clink
WHUMP
GAK!

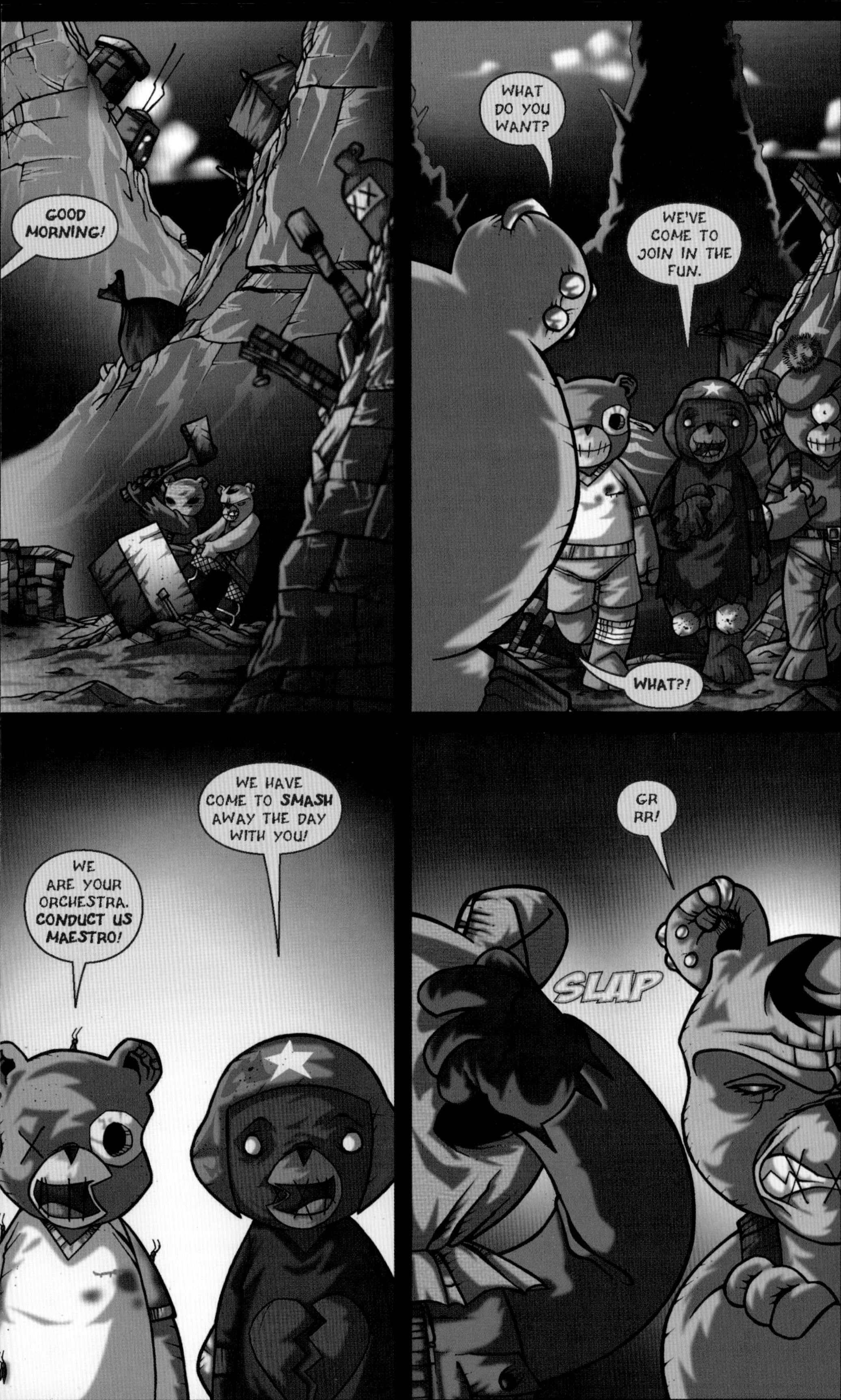
GOOD MORNING!
WHAT DO YOU WANT?
WE'VE COME TO JOIN IN THE FUN.
WHAT?!
WE HAVE COME TO SMASH AWAY THE DAY WITH YOU!
WE ARE YOUR ORCHESTRA. CONDUCT US MAESTRO!
GR RR!
SLAP

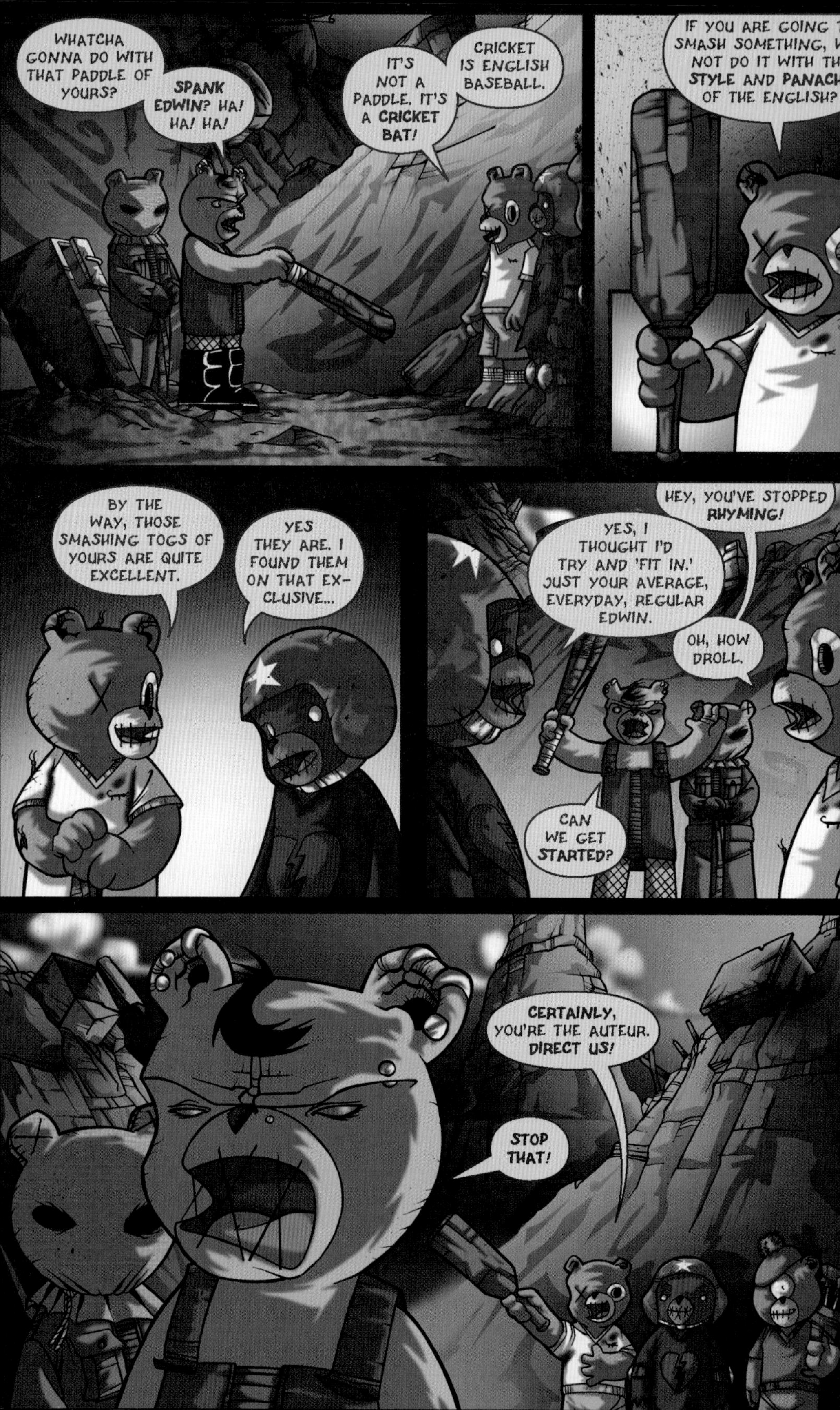
WHATCHA GONNA DO WITH THAT PADDLE OF YOURS?
SPANK EDWIN? HA! HA! HA!
IT'S NOT A PADDLE. IT'S A CRICKET BAT!
CRICKET IS ENGLISH BASEBALL.
IF YOU ARE GOING T SMASH SOMETHING, W NOT DO IT WITH TH STYLE AND PANACH OF THE ENGLISH?
BY THE WAY, THOSE SMASHING TOGS OF YOURS ARE QUITE EXCELLENT.
YES THEY ARE. I FOUND THEM ON THAT EX-CLUSIVE...
HEY, YOU'VE STOPPED RHYMING!
YES, I THOUGHT I'D TRY AND 'FIT IN.' JUST YOUR AVERAGE, EVERYDAY, REGULAR EDWIN.
OH, HOW DROLL.
CAN WE GET STARTED?
CERTAINLY, YOU'RE THE AUTEUR. DIRECT US!
STOP THAT!

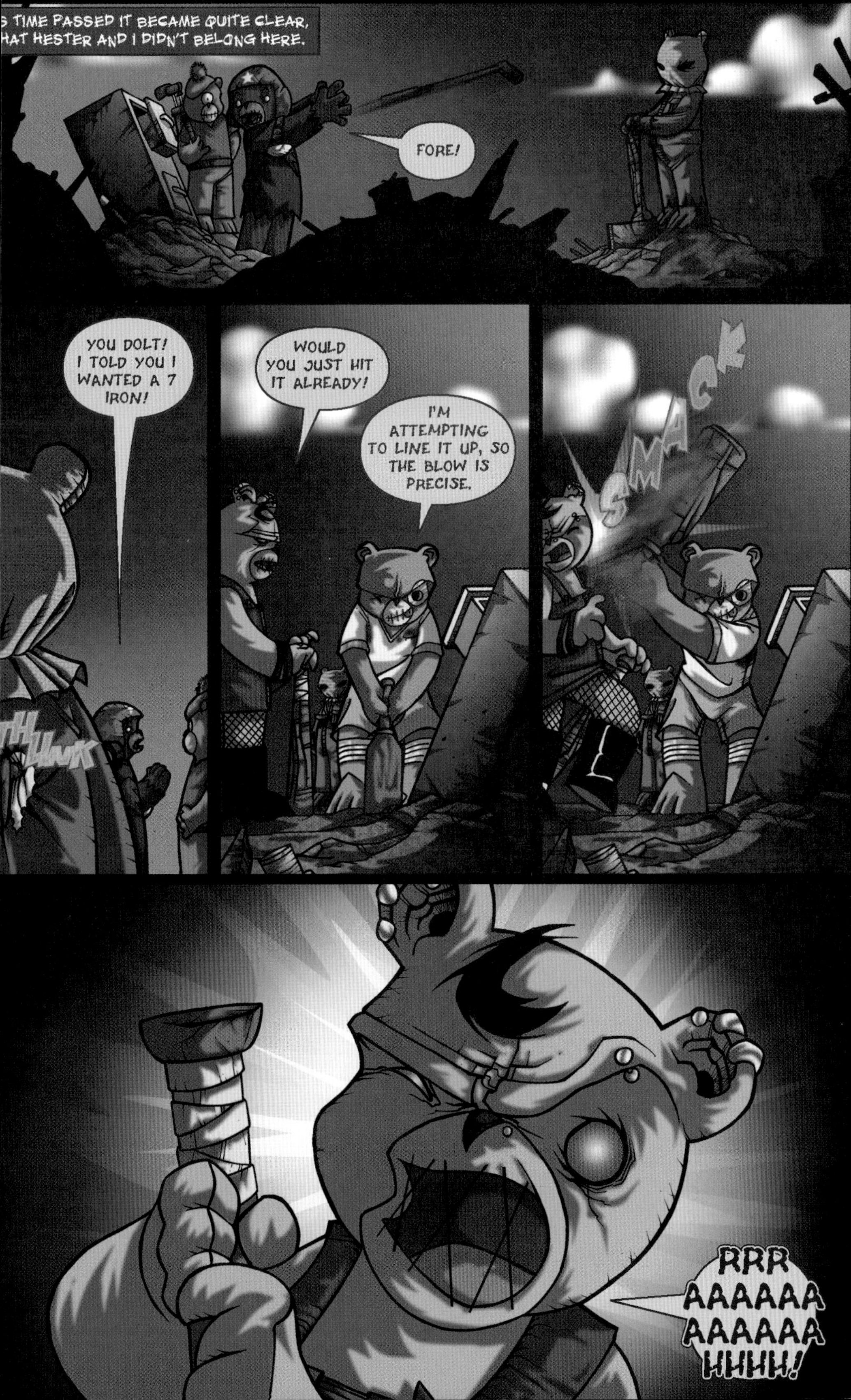
S TIME PASSED IT BECAME QUITE CLEAR,
HAT HESTER AND I DIDN'T BELONG HERE.
FORE!
YOU DOLT! I TOLD YOU I WANTED A 7 IRON!
THUNK
WOULD YOU JUST HIT IT ALREADY!
I'M ATTEMPTING TO LINE IT UP, SO THE BLOW IS PRECISE.
SMACK
RRRAAAAAAAAAAAAHHHH!

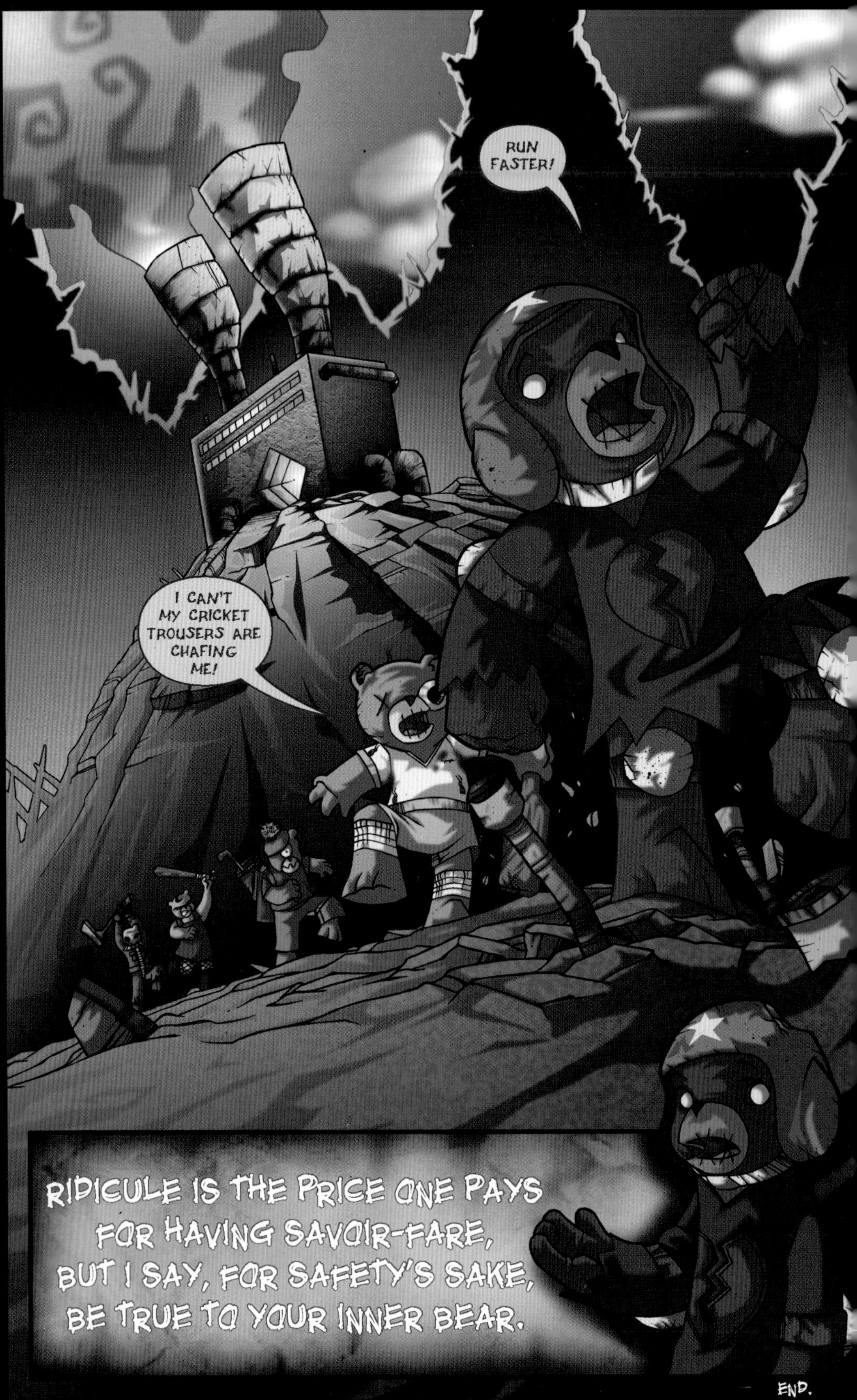
RUN FASTER!
I CAN'T MY CRICKET TROUSERS ARE CHAFING ME!
RIDICULE IS THE PRICE ONE PAYS FOR HAVING SAVOIR-FARE, BUT I SAY, FOR SAFETY'S SAKE, BE TRUE TO YOUR INNER BEAR.
END.

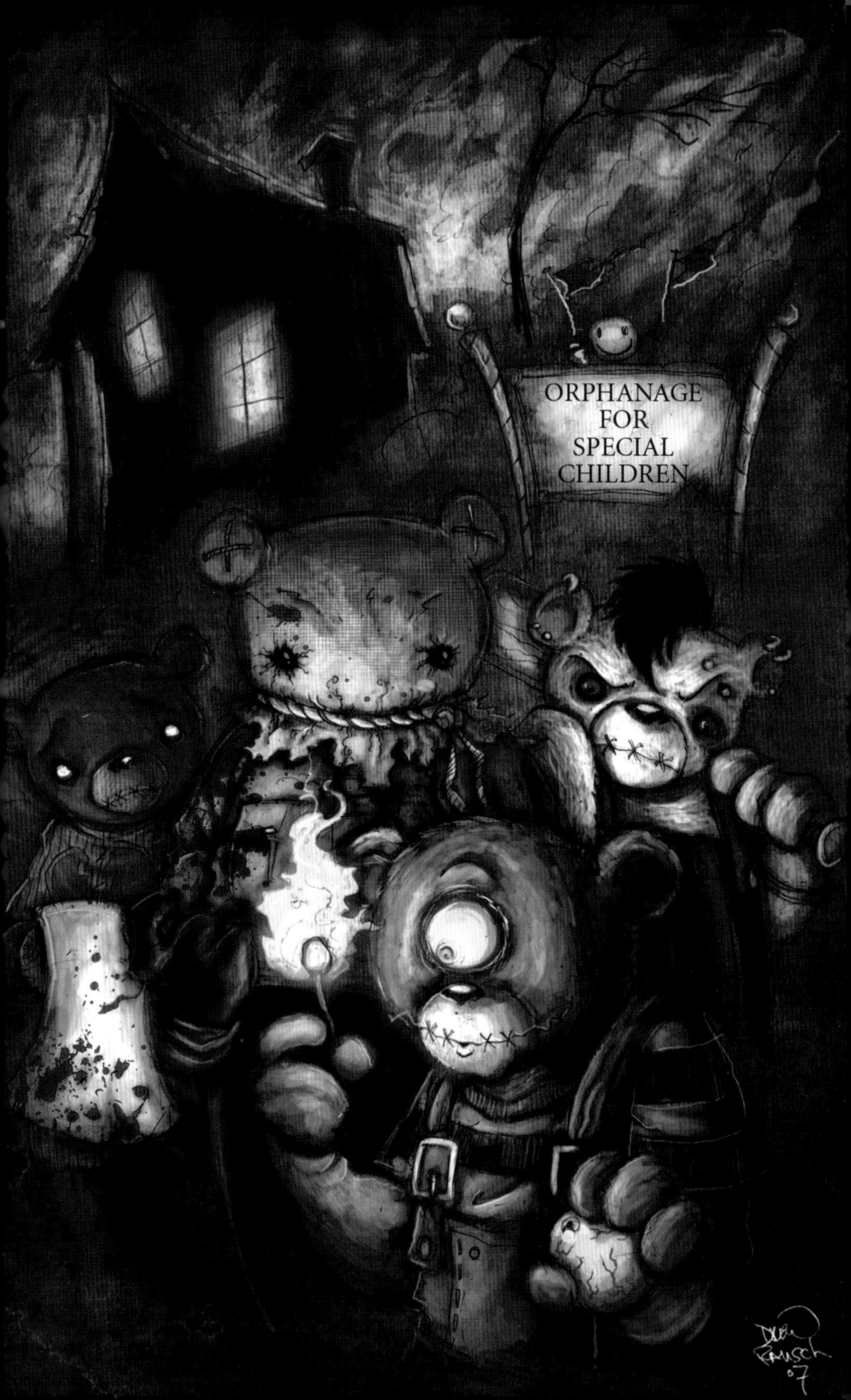
ORPHANAGE
FOR
SPECIAL
CHILDREN

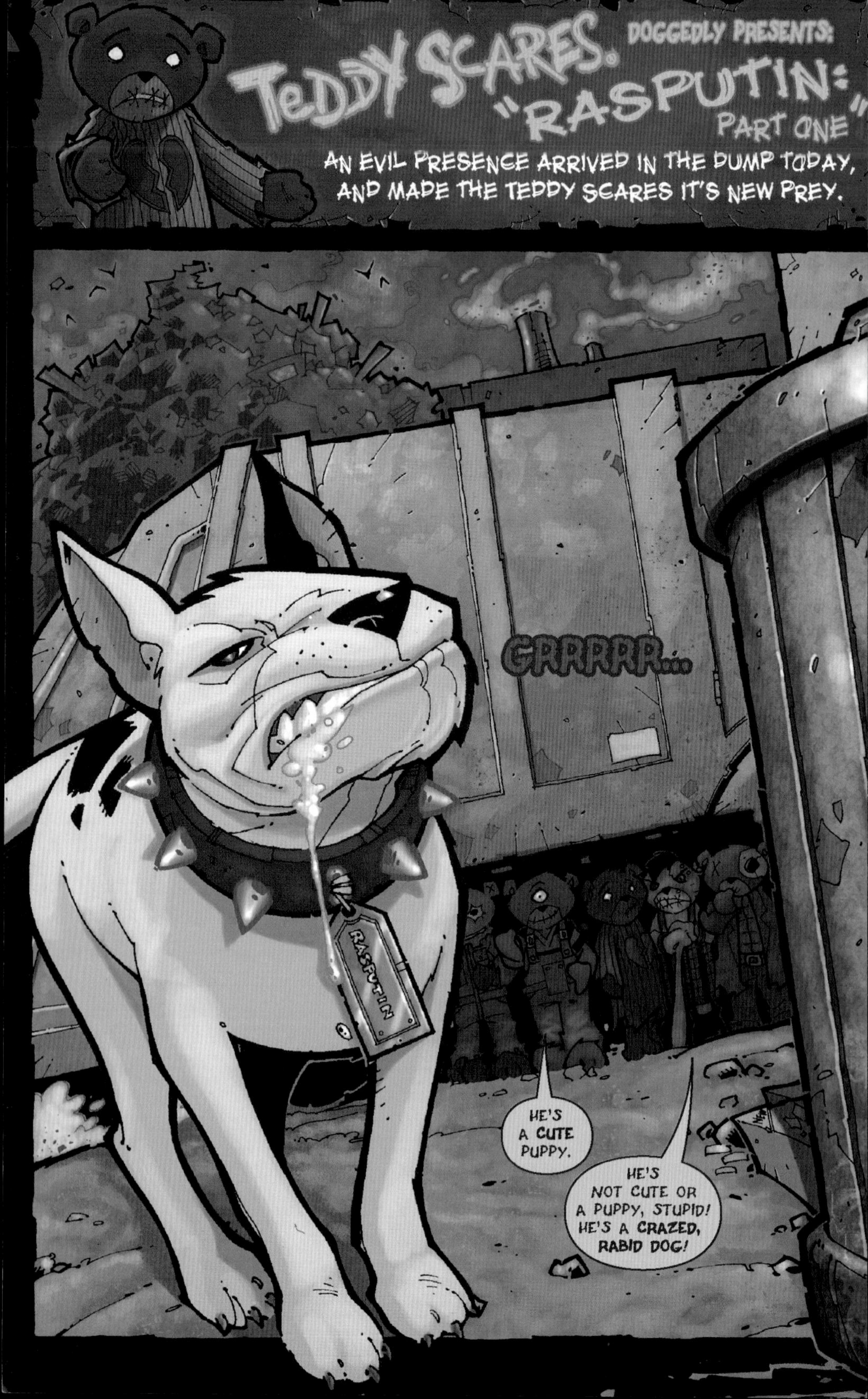
TEDDY SCARES.
DOGGEDLY PRESENTS:
"RASPUTIN:"
PART ONE
AN EVIL PRESENCE ARRIVED IN THE DUMP TODAY, AND MADE THE TEDDY SCARES IT'S NEW PREY.
GRRRRR...
RASPUTIN
HE'S A CUTE PUPPY.
HE'S NOT CUTE OR A PUPPY, STUPID! HE'S A CRAZED, RABID DOG!

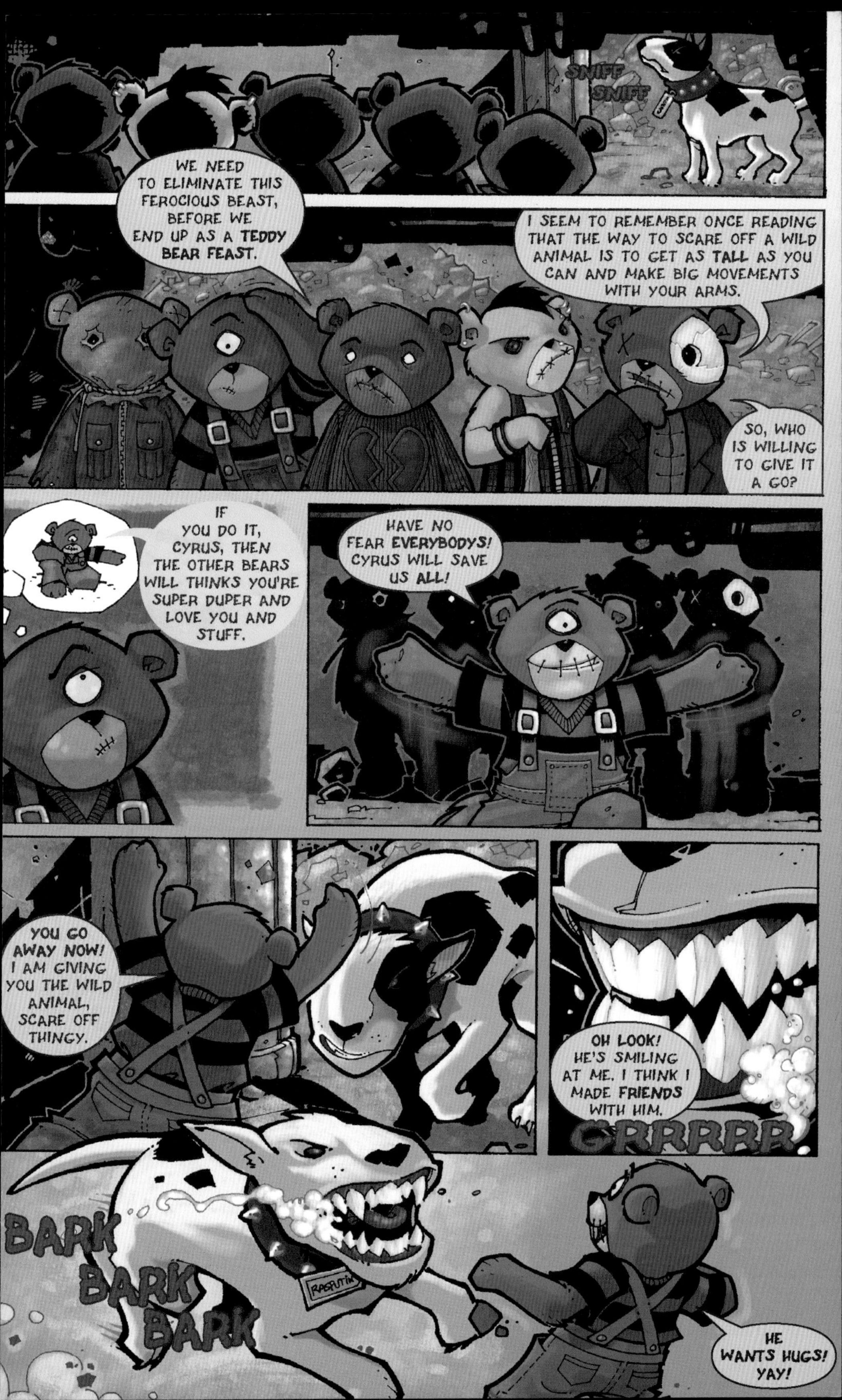

SNIFF
SNIFF
WE NEED TO ELIMINATE THIS FEROCIOUS BEAST, BEFORE WE END UP AS A TEDDY BEAR FEAST.
I SEEM TO REMEMBER ONCE READING THAT THE WAY TO SCARE OFF A WILD ANIMAL IS TO GET AS TALL AS YOU CAN AND MAKE BIG MOVEMENTS WITH YOUR ARMS.
SO, WHO IS WILLING TO GIVE IT A GO?
IF YOU DO IT, CYRUS, THEN THE OTHER BEARS WILL THINKS YOU'RE SUPER DUPER AND LOVE YOU AND STUFF.
HAVE NO FEAR EVERYBODYS! CYRUS WILL SAVE US ALL!
YOU GO AWAY NOW! I AM GIVING YOU THE WILD ANIMAL, SCARE OFF THINGY.
OH LOOK! HE'S SMILING AT ME. I THINK I MADE FRIENDS WITH HIM.
GRRRRR
BARK
BARK
BARK
RASPUTIN
HE WANTS HUGS! YAY!

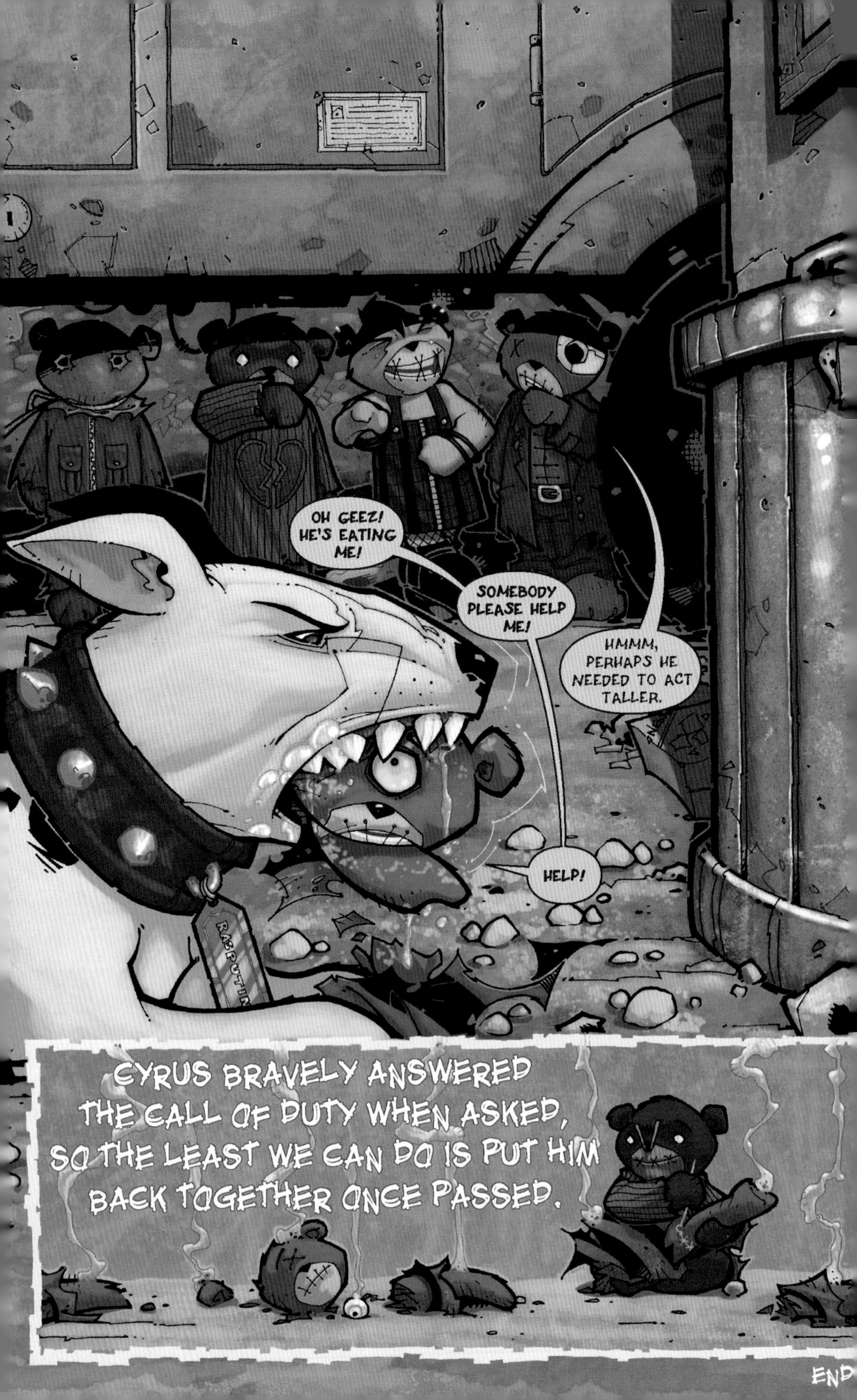
OH GEEZ! HE'S EATING ME!
SOMEBODY PLEASE HELP ME!
HMMM, PERHAPS HE NEEDED TO ACT TALLER.
HELP!
RASPUTIN
CYRUS BRAVELY ANSWERED THE CALL OF DUTY WHEN ASKED, SO THE LEAST WE CAN DO IS PUT HIM BACK TOGETHER ONCE PASSED.
END

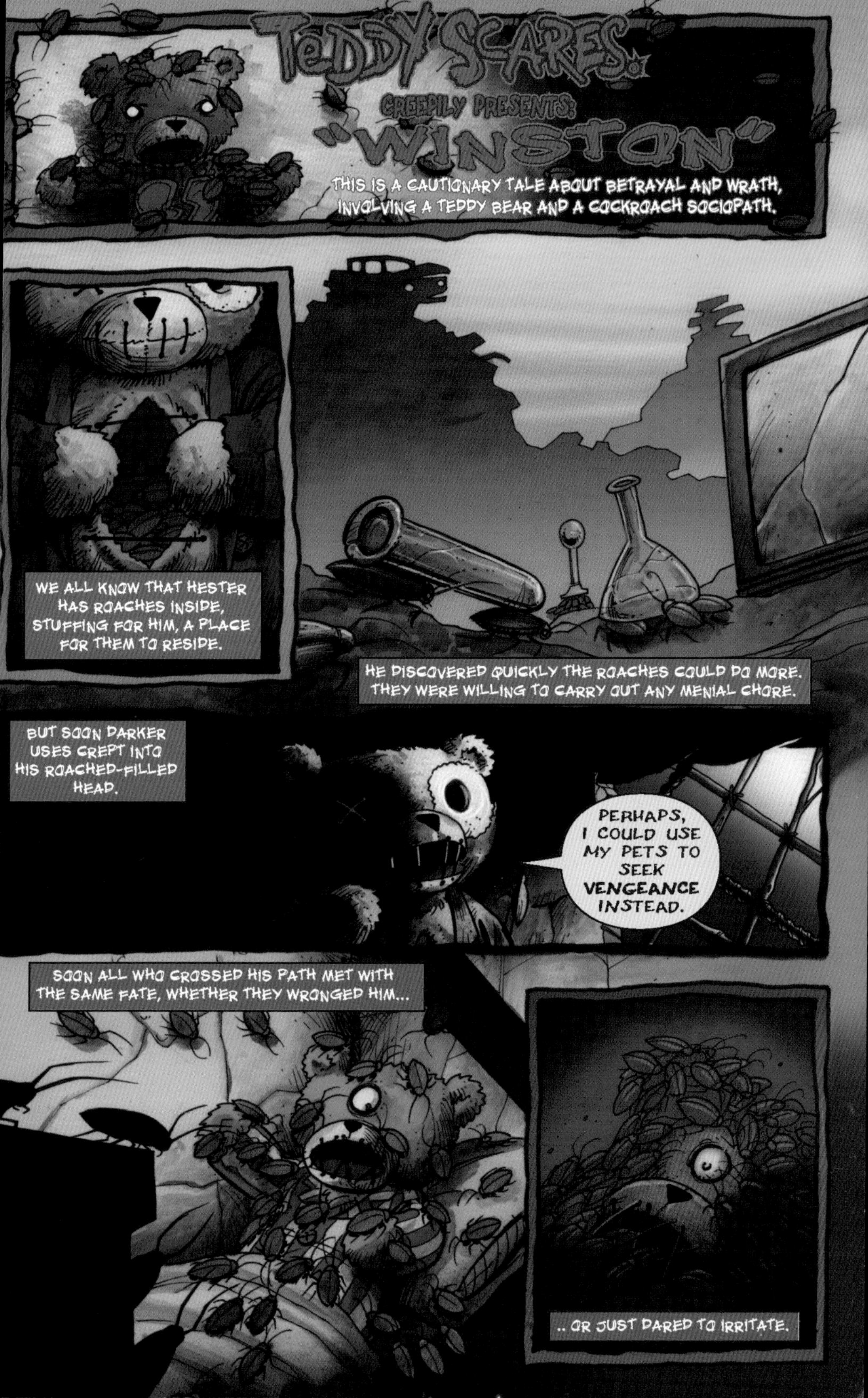
TEDDY SCARES
CREEPILY PRESENTS:
"WINSTON"
THIS IS A CAUTIONARY TALE ABOUT BETRAYAL AND WRATH, INVOLVING A TEDDY BEAR AND A COCKROACH SOCIOPATH.
WE ALL KNOW THAT HESTER HAS ROACHES INSIDE, STUFFING FOR HIM, A PLACE FOR THEM TO RESIDE.
HE DISCOVERED QUICKLY THE ROACHES COULD DO MORE. THEY WERE WILLING TO CARRY OUT ANY MENIAL CHORE.
BUT SOON DARKER USES CREPT INTO HIS ROACHED-FILLED HEAD.
PERHAPS, I COULD USE MY PETS TO SEEK VENGEANCE INSTEAD.
SOON ALL WHO CROSSED HIS PATH MET WITH THE SAME FATE, WHETHER THEY WRONGED HIM...
.. OR JUST DARED TO IRRITATE.

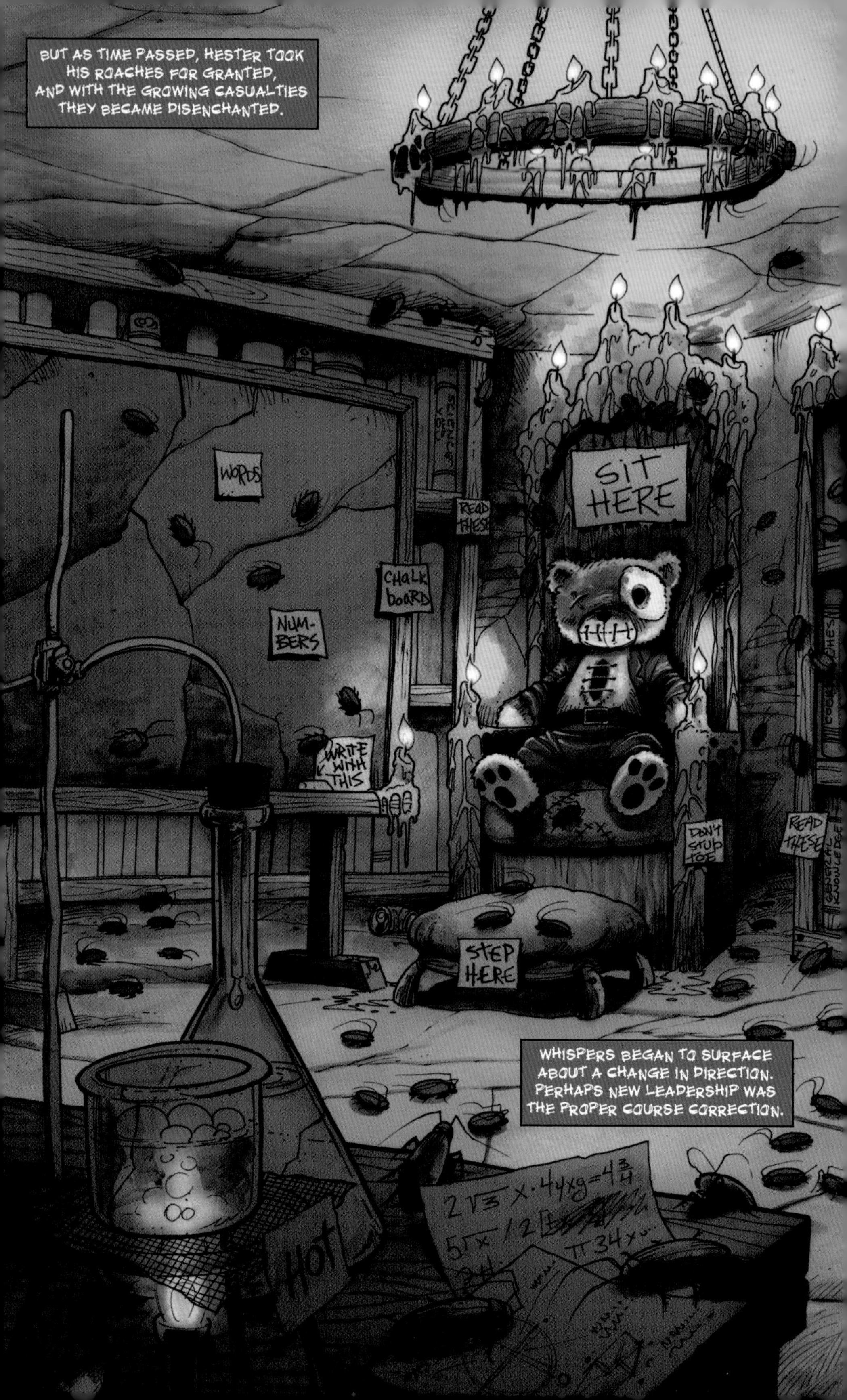

BUT AS TIME PASSED, HESTER TOOK HIS ROACHES FOR GRANTED, AND WITH THE GROWING CASUALTIES THEY BECAME DISENCHANTED.
WORDS
READ THESE
SIT HERE
CHALK board
NUM-BERS
WRITE WITH THIS
READ THESE
STEP HERE
HOT
WHISPERS BEGAN TO SURFACE ABOUT A CHANGE IN DIRECTION. PERHAPS NEW LEADERSHIP WAS THE PROPER COURSE CORRECTION.

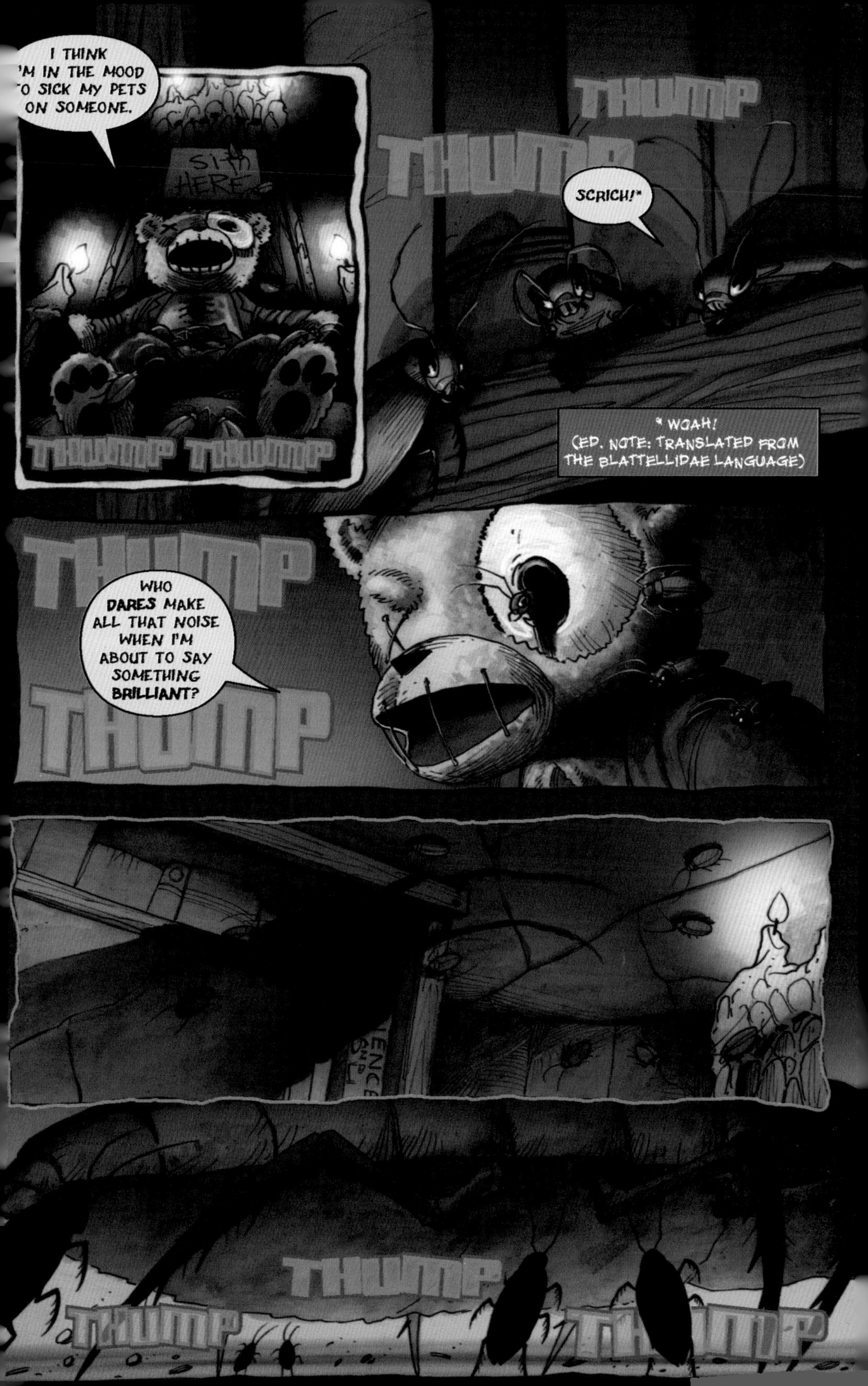
I THINK I'M IN THE MOOD TO SICK MY PETS ON SOMEONE.
SIT HERE
THUMP THUMP
THUMP
THUMP
SCRICH!*
* WOAH! (ED. NOTE: TRANSLATED FROM THE BLATTELLIDAE LANGUAGE)
THUMP
WHO DARES MAKE ALL THAT NOISE WHEN I'M ABOUT TO SAY SOMETHING BRILLIANT?
THUMP
THUMP
THUMP
THUMP

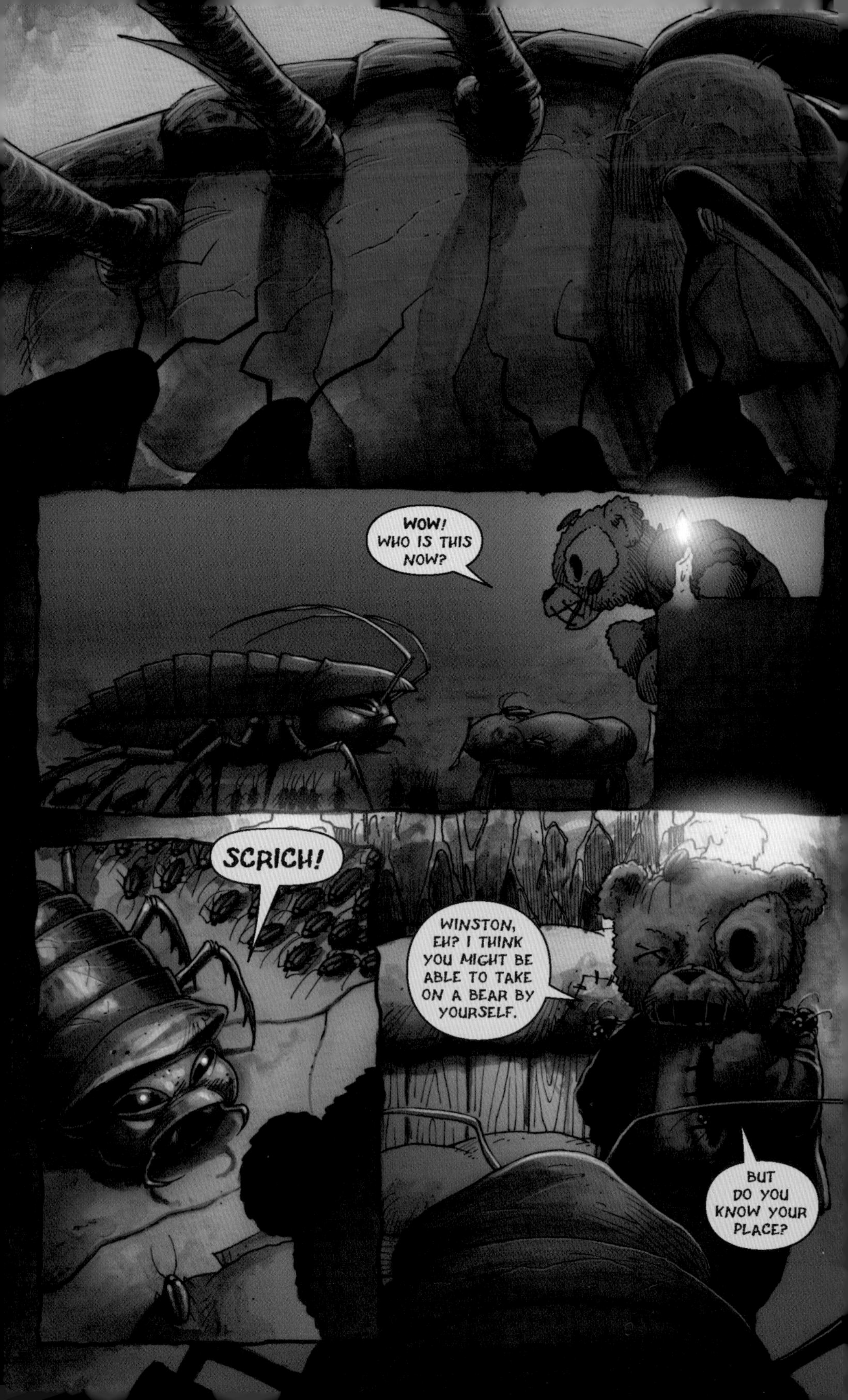
WOW! WHO IS THIS NOW?
SCRICH!
WINSTON, EH? I THINK YOU MIGHT BE ABLE TO TAKE ON A BEAR BY YOURSELF.
BUT DO YOU KNOW YOUR PLACE?

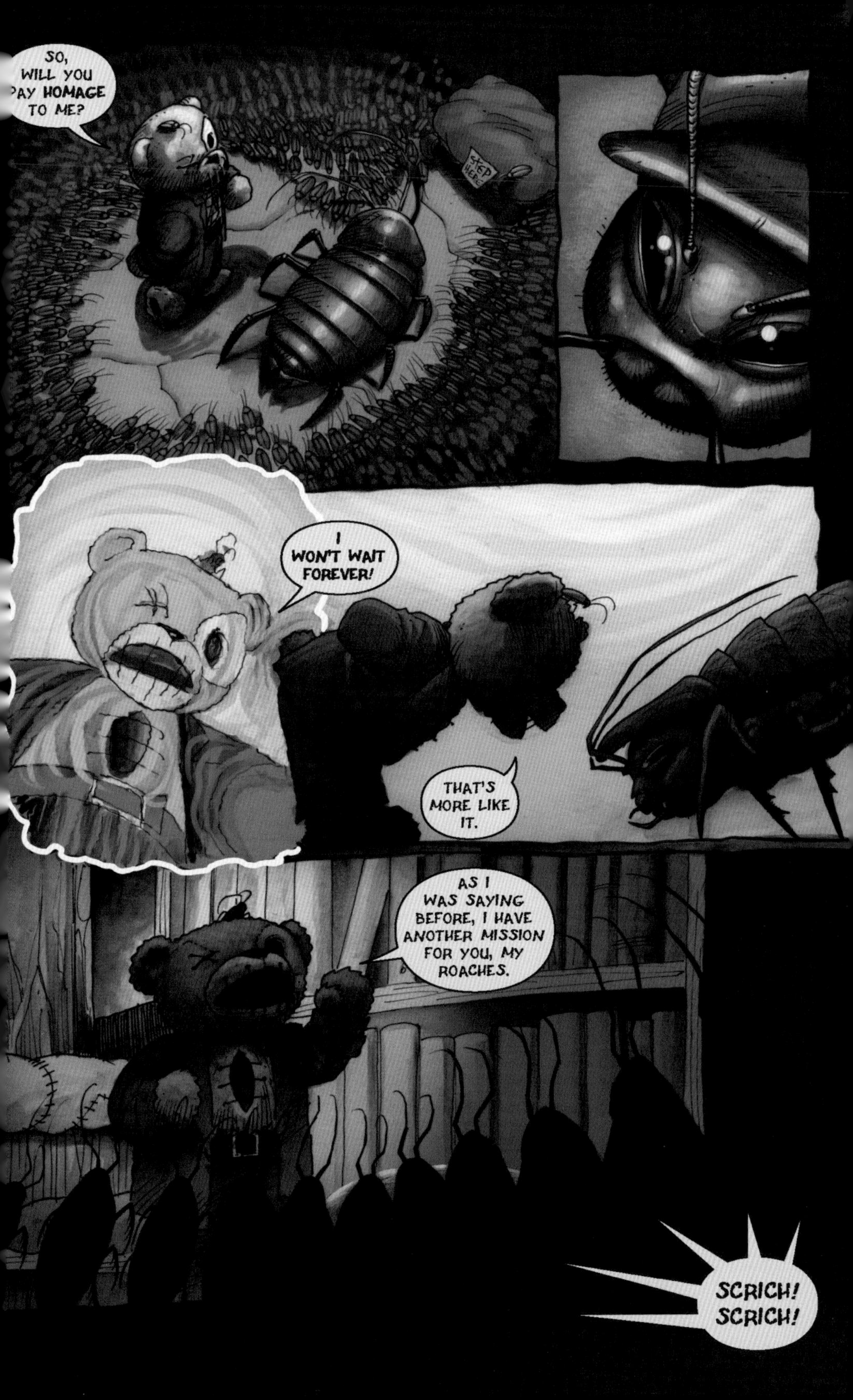
SO, WILL YOU PAY HOMAGE TO ME?
STEP HERE
I WON'T WAIT FOREVER!
THAT'S MORE LIKE IT.
AS I WAS SAYING BEFORE, I HAVE ANOTHER MISSION FOR YOU, MY ROACHES.
SCRICH! SCRICH!

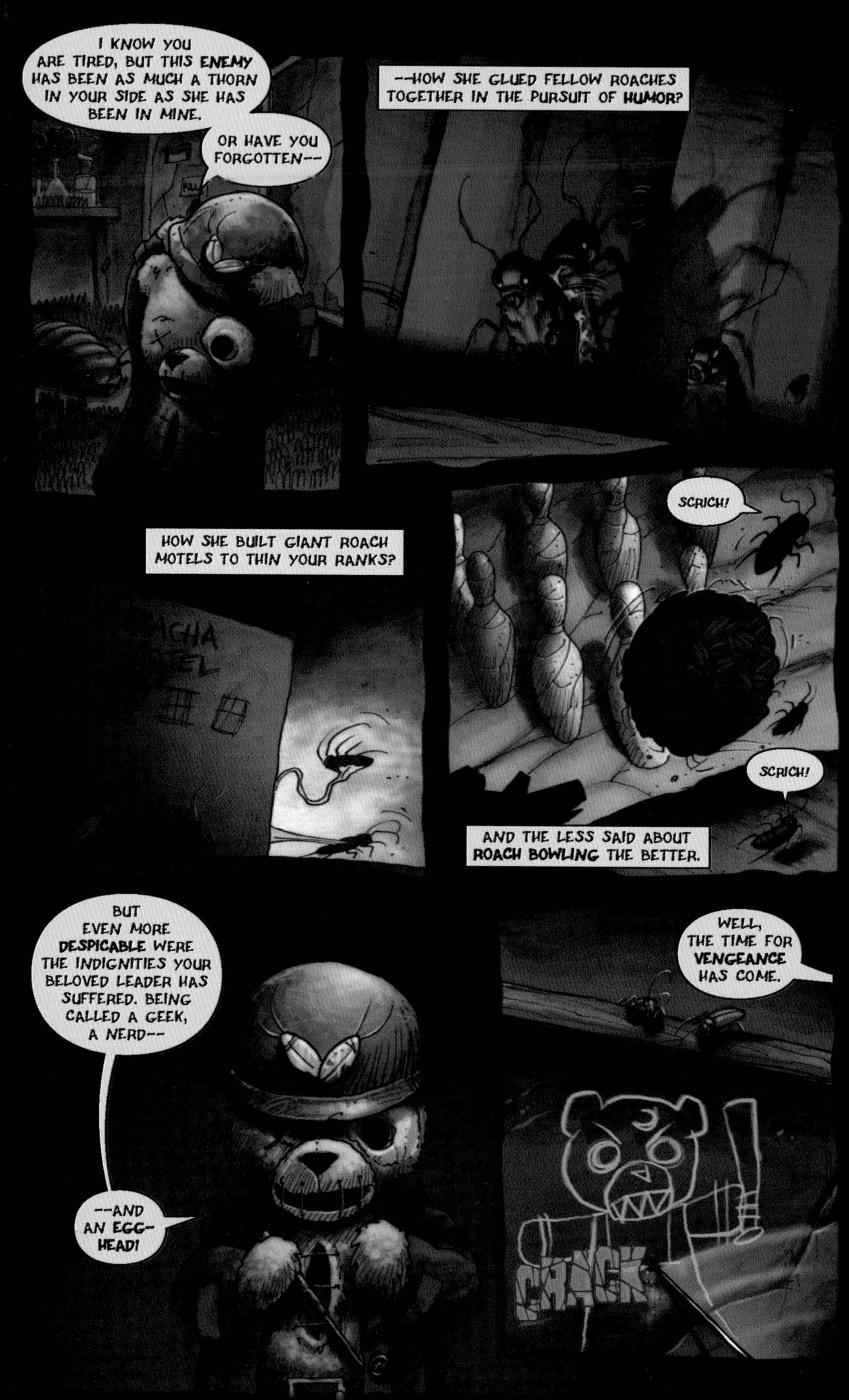
I KNOW YOU ARE TIRED, BUT THIS ENEMY HAS BEEN AS MUCH A THORN IN YOUR SIDE AS SHE HAS BEEN IN MINE.
OR HAVE YOU FORGOTTEN--
--HOW SHE GLUED FELLOW ROACHES TOGETHER IN THE PURSUIT OF HUMOR?
HOW SHE BUILT GIANT ROACH MOTELS TO THIN YOUR RANKS?
SCRICH!
SCRICH!
AND THE LESS SAID ABOUT ROACH BOWLING THE BETTER.
BUT EVEN MORE DESPICABLE WERE THE INDIGNITIES YOUR BELOVED LEADER HAS SUFFERED. BEING CALLED A GEEK, A NERD--
--AND AN EGG-HEAD!
WELL, THE TIME FOR VENGEANCE HAS COME.
CRACK

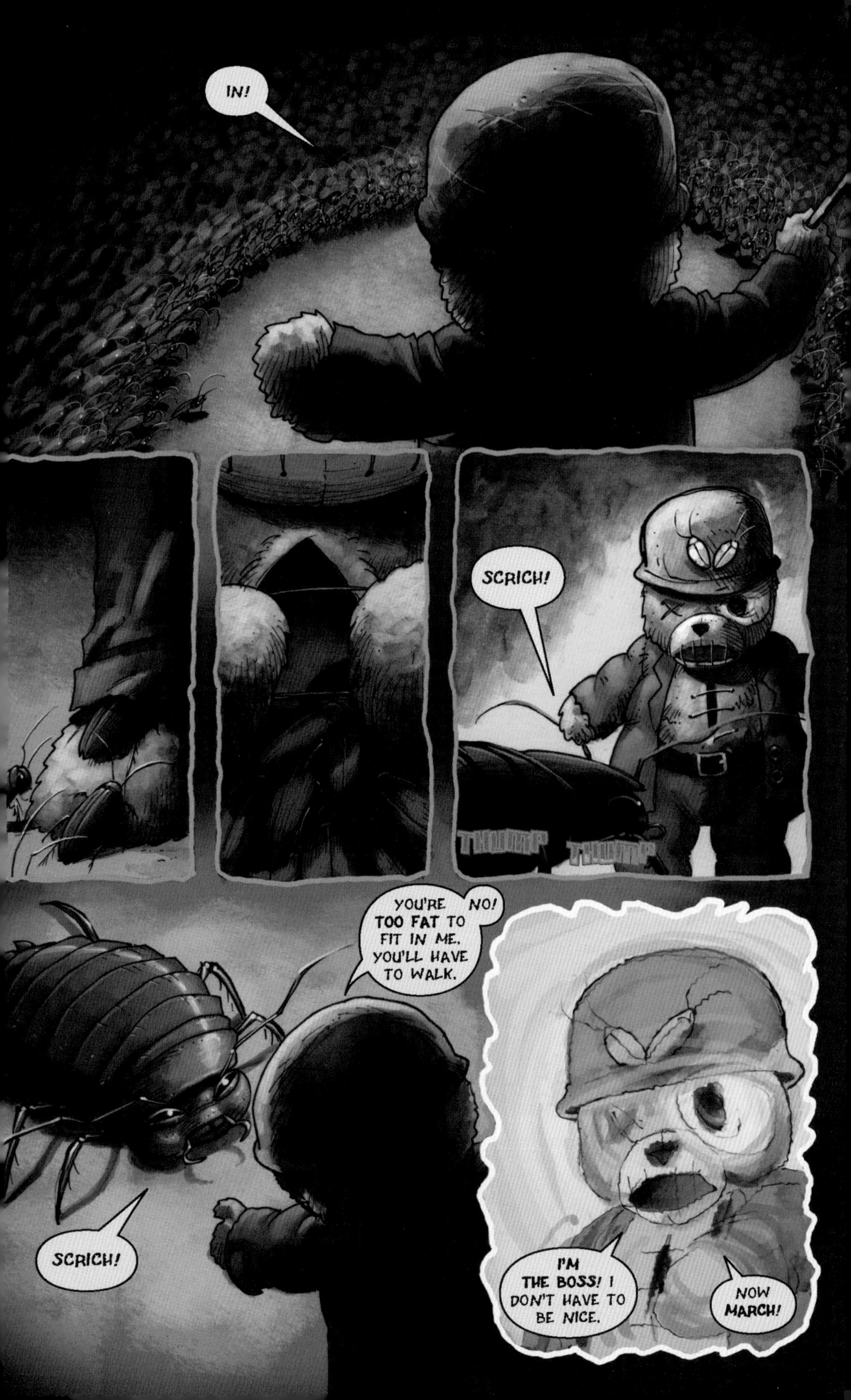
IN!
SCRICH!
THUMP THUMP
YOU'RE TOO FAT TO FIT IN ME. YOU'LL HAVE TO WALK.
NO!
SCRICH!
I'M THE BOSS! I DON'T HAVE TO BE NICE.
NOW MARCH!

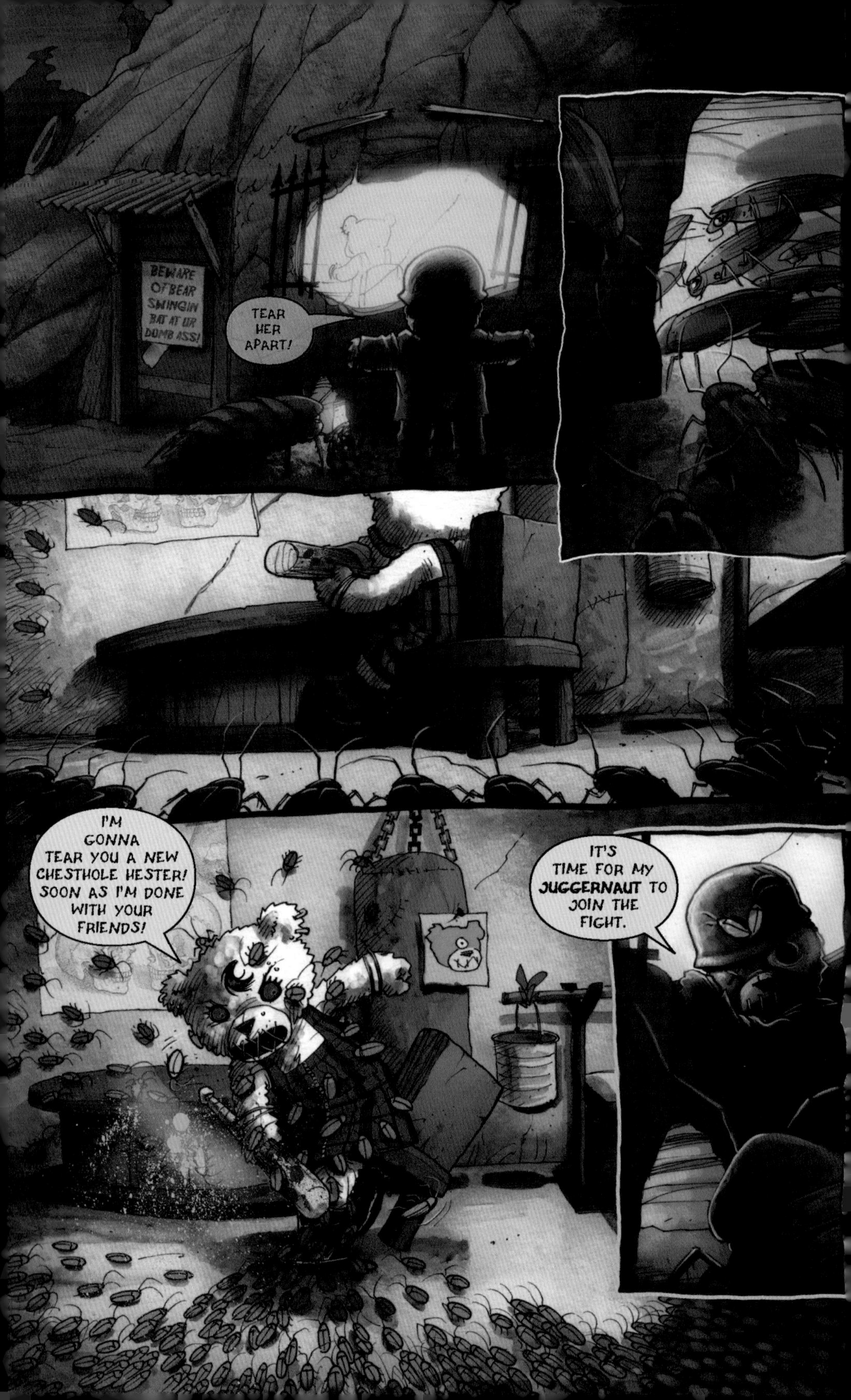
BEWARE OF BEAR SWINGIN BAT AT UR DUMB ASS!
TEAR HER APART!
I'M GONNA TEAR YOU A NEW CHESTHOLE HESTER! SOON AS I'M DONE WITH YOUR FRIENDS!
IT'S TIME FOR MY **JUGGERNAUT** TO JOIN THE FIGHT.

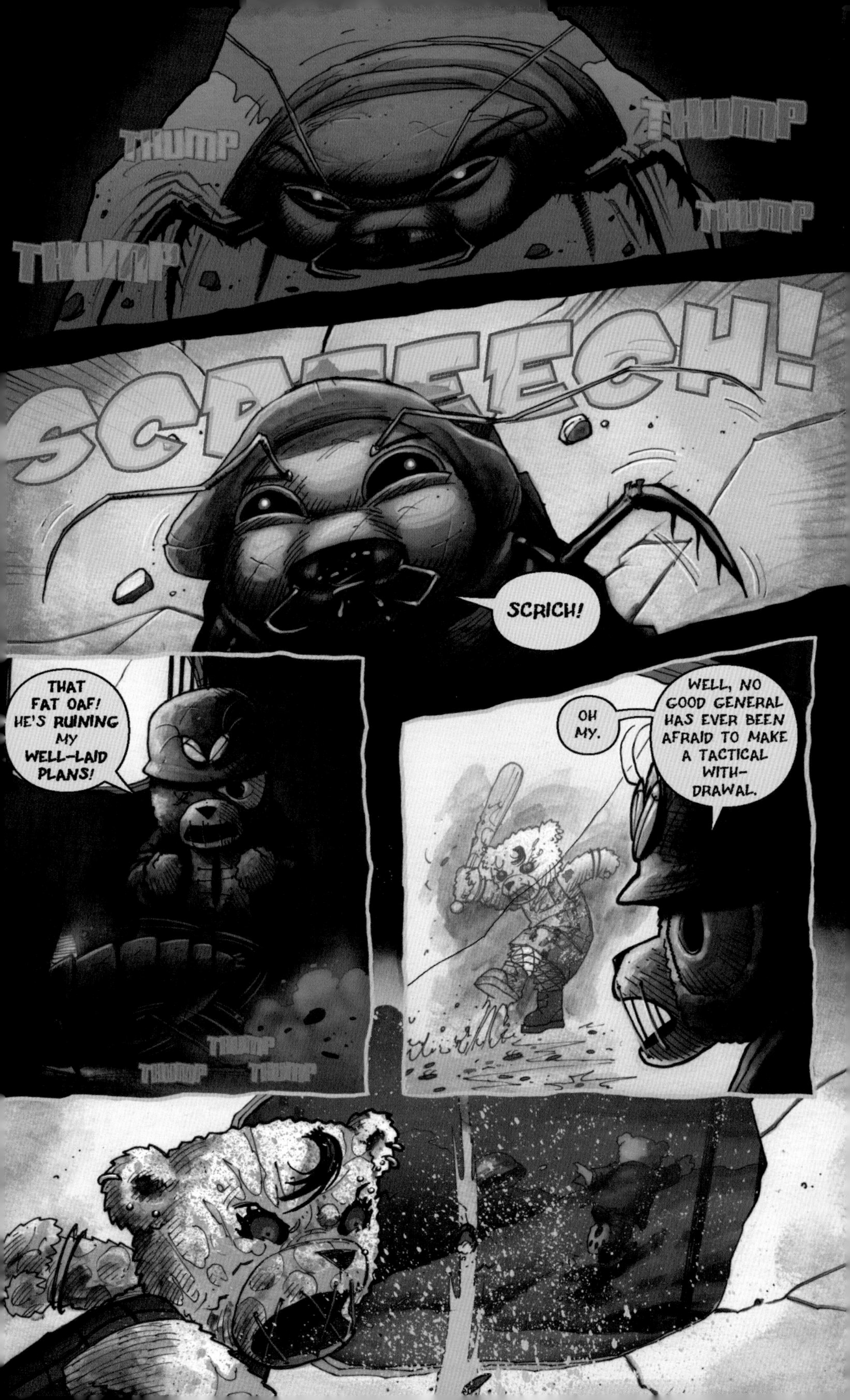
THUMP
THUMP
THUMP
THUMP
SCREECH!
SCRICH!
THAT FAT OAF! HE'S RUINING MY WELL-LAID PLANS!
THUMP
THUMP
THUMP
OH MY.
WELL, NO GOOD GENERAL HAS EVER BEEN AFRAID TO MAKE A TACTICAL WITH-DRAWAL.

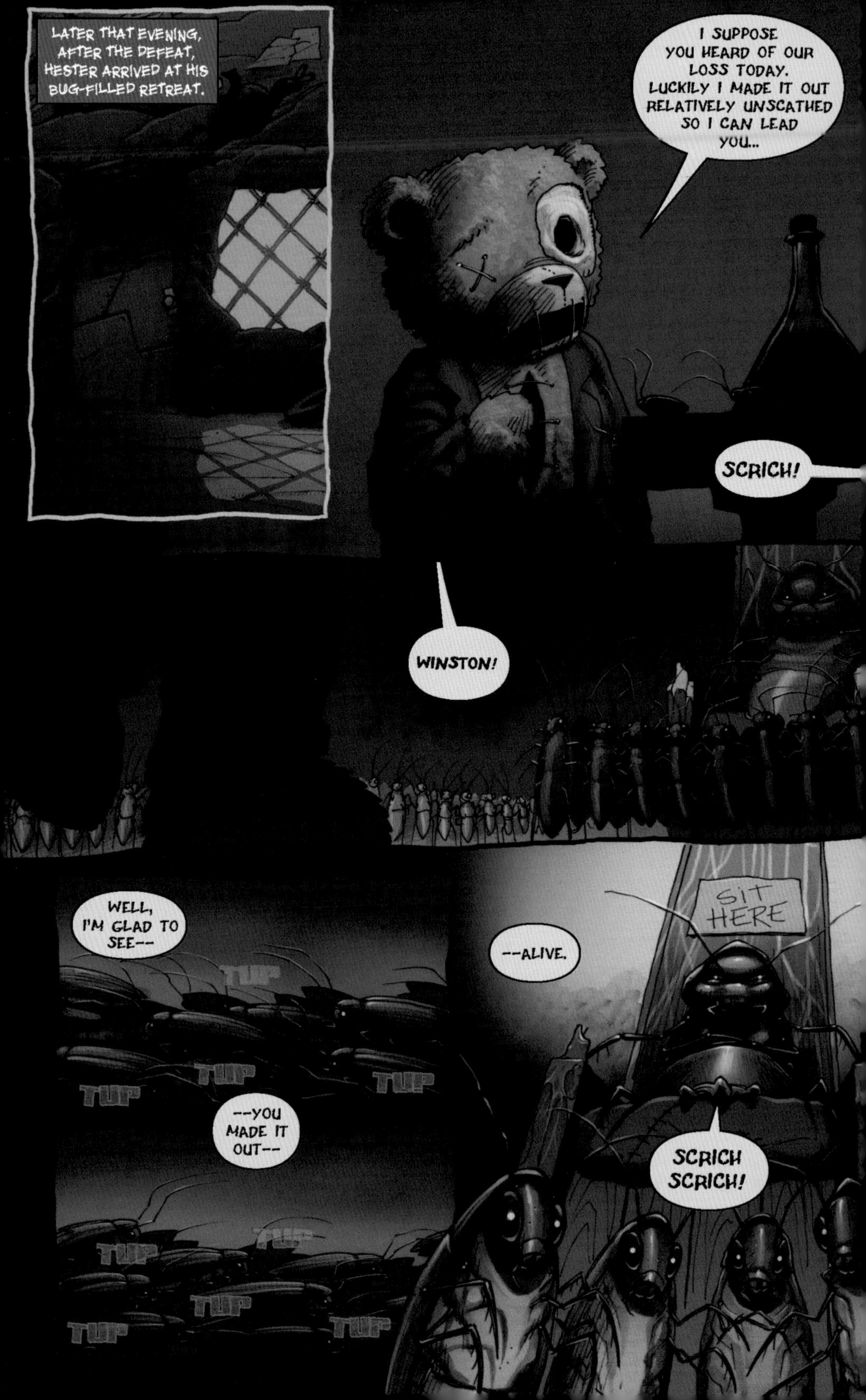
LATER THAT EVENING, AFTER THE DEFEAT, HESTER ARRIVED AT HIS BUG-FILLED RETREAT.
I SUPPOSE YOU HEARD OF OUR LOSS TODAY. LUCKILY I MADE IT OUT RELATIVELY UNSCATHED SO I CAN LEAD YOU...
SCRICH!
WINSTON!
WELL, I'M GLAD TO SEE--
--ALIVE.
SIT HERE
TUP
TUP
TUP
TUP
--YOU MADE IT OUT--
SCRICH SCRICH!
TUP
TUP
TUP
TUP
TUP

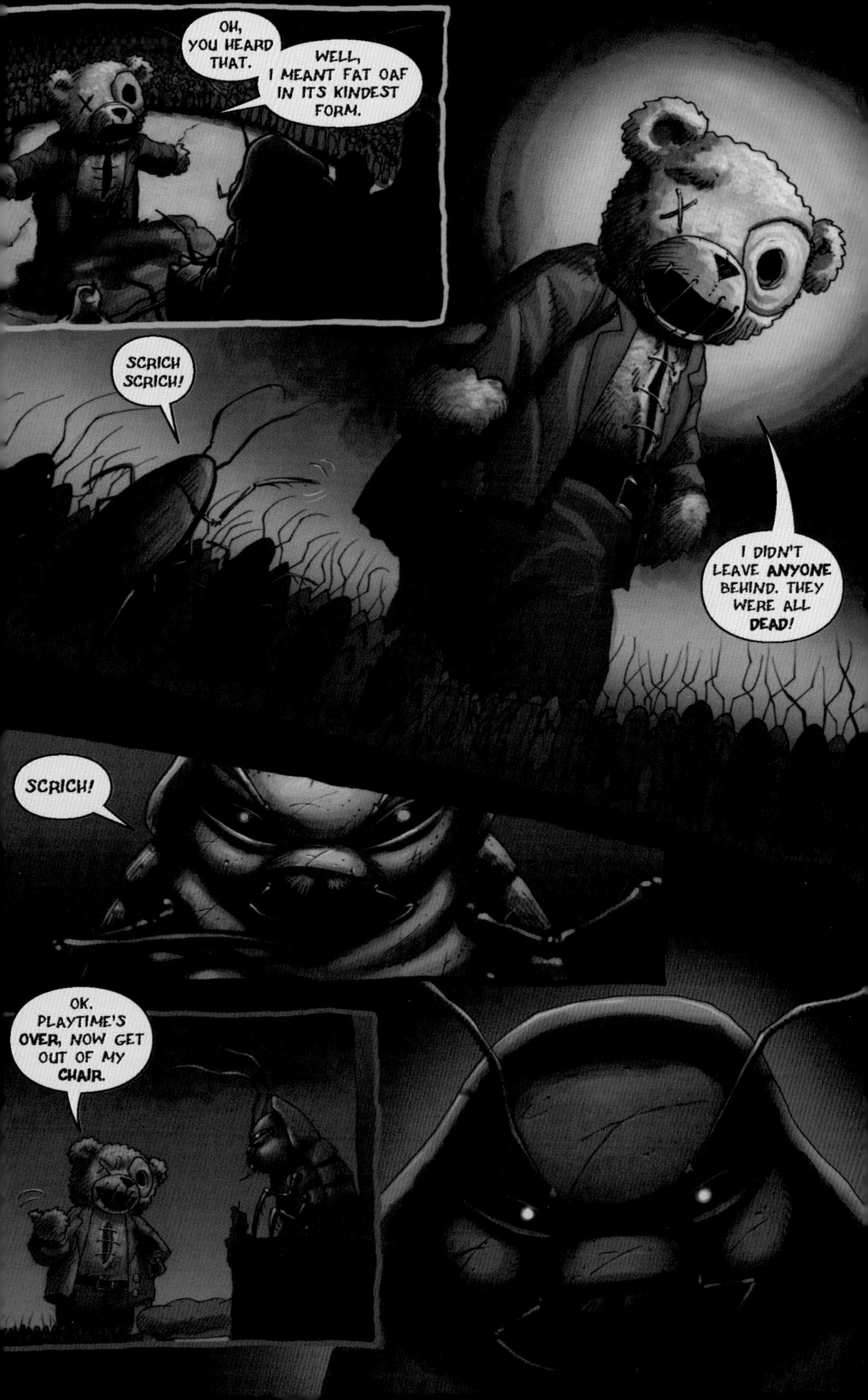
OH, YOU HEARD THAT.
WELL, I MEANT FAT OAF IN ITS KINDEST FORM.
SCRICH SCRICH!
I DIDN'T LEAVE ANYONE BEHIND. THEY WERE ALL DEAD!
SCRICH!
OK. PLAYTIME'S OVER, NOW GET OUT OF MY CHAIR.

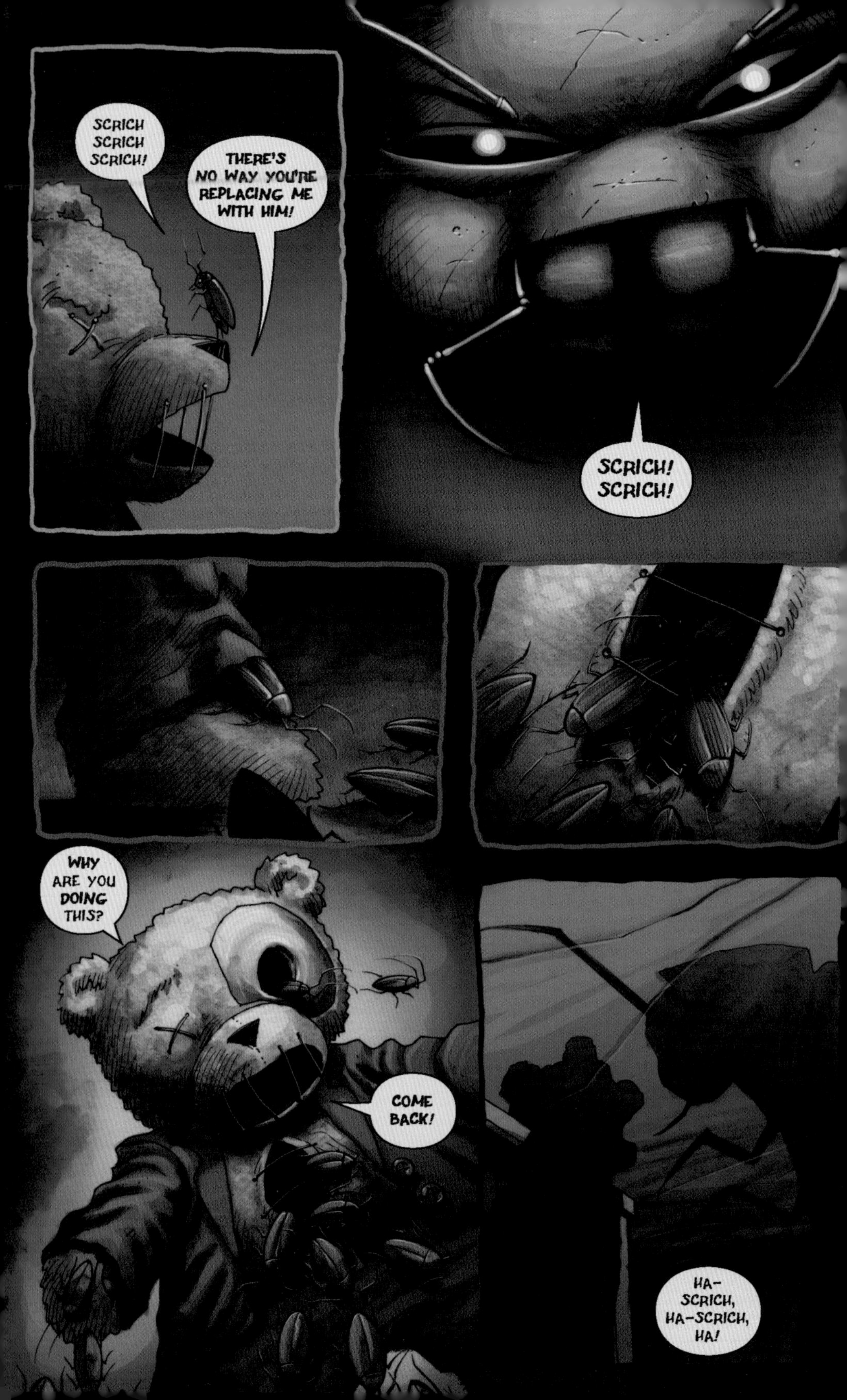
SCRICH SCRICH SCRICH!
THERE'S NO WAY YOU'RE REPLACING ME WITH HIM!
SCRICH! SCRICH!
WHY ARE YOU DOING THIS?
COME BACK!
HA-SCRICH, HA-SCRICH, HA!

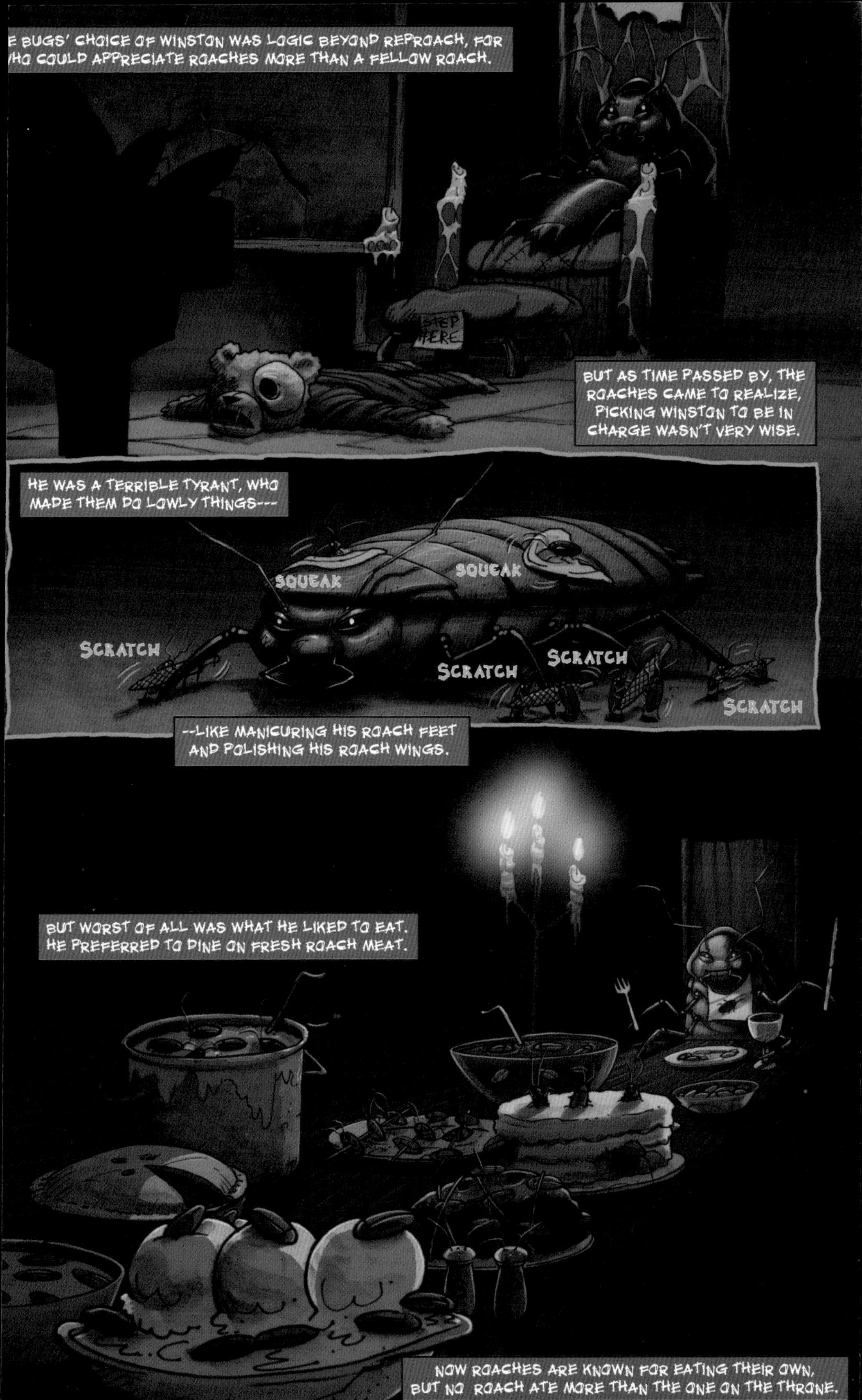
E BUGS' CHOICE OF WINSTON WAS LOGIC BEYOND REPROACH, FOR
HO COULD APPRECIATE ROACHES MORE THAN A FELLOW ROACH.
STEP HERE
BUT AS TIME PASSED BY, THE ROACHES CAME TO REALIZE, PICKING WINSTON TO BE IN CHARGE WASN'T VERY WISE.
HE WAS A TERRIBLE TYRANT, WHO MADE THEM DO LOWLY THINGS---
SQUEAK
SQUEAK
SCRATCH
SCRATCH
SCRATCH
SCRATCH
--LIKE MANICURING HIS ROACH FEET AND POLISHING HIS ROACH WINGS.
BUT WORST OF ALL WAS WHAT HE LIKED TO EAT.
HE PREFERRED TO DINE ON FRESH ROACH MEAT.
NOW ROACHES ARE KNOWN FOR EATING THEIR OWN,
BUT NO ROACH ATE MORE THAN THE ONE ON THE THRONE.

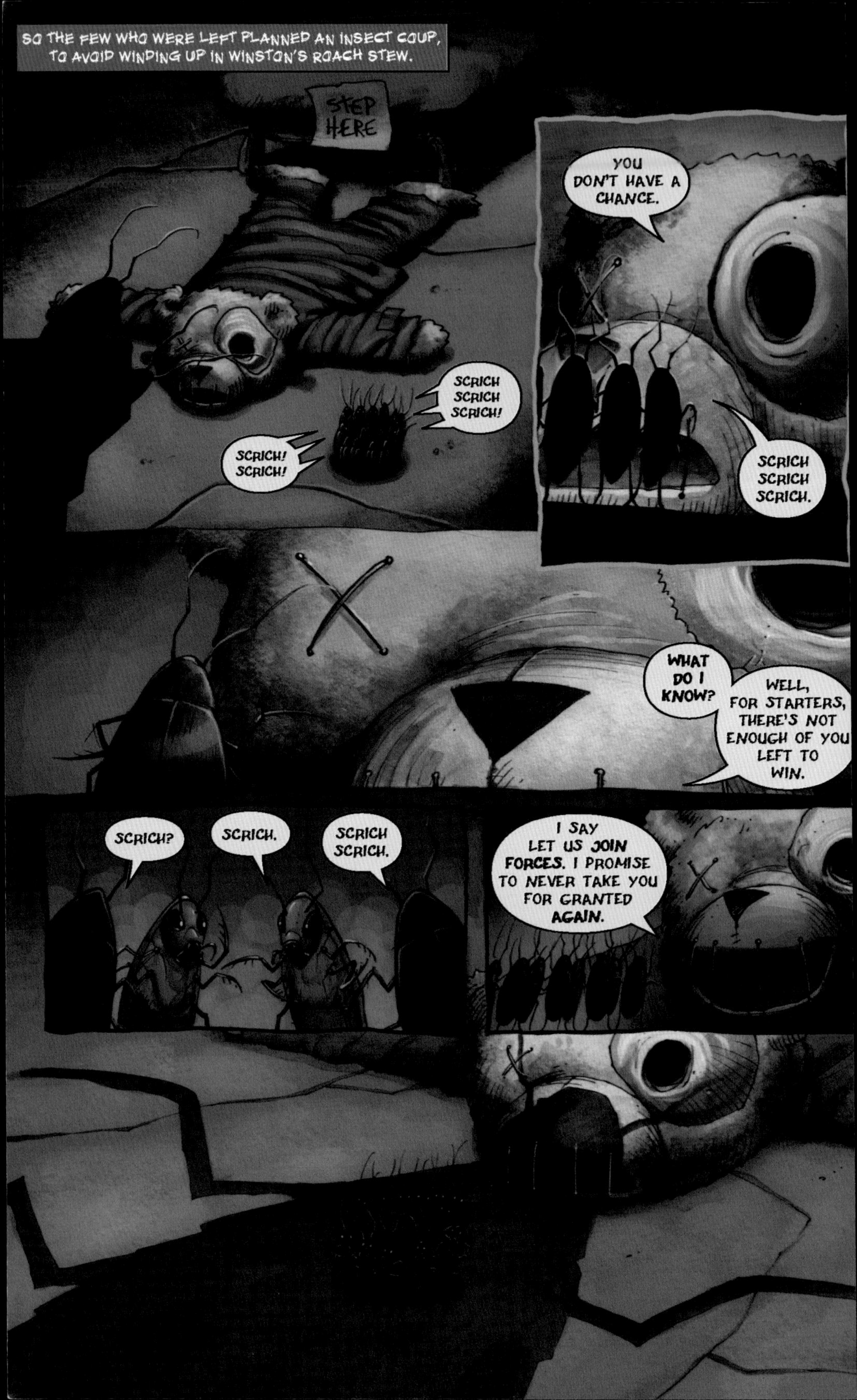
SO THE FEW WHO WERE LEFT PLANNED AN INSECT COUP,
TO AVOID WINDING UP IN WINSTON'S ROACH STEW.
STEP HERE
SCRICH SCRICH SCRICH!
SCRICH! SCRICH!
YOU DON'T HAVE A CHANCE.
SCRICH SCRICH SCRICH.
WHAT DO I KNOW?
WELL, FOR STARTERS, THERE'S NOT ENOUGH OF YOU LEFT TO WIN.
SCRICH?
SCRICH.
SCRICH SCRICH.
I SAY LET US JOIN FORCES. I PROMISE TO NEVER TAKE YOU FOR GRANTED AGAIN.

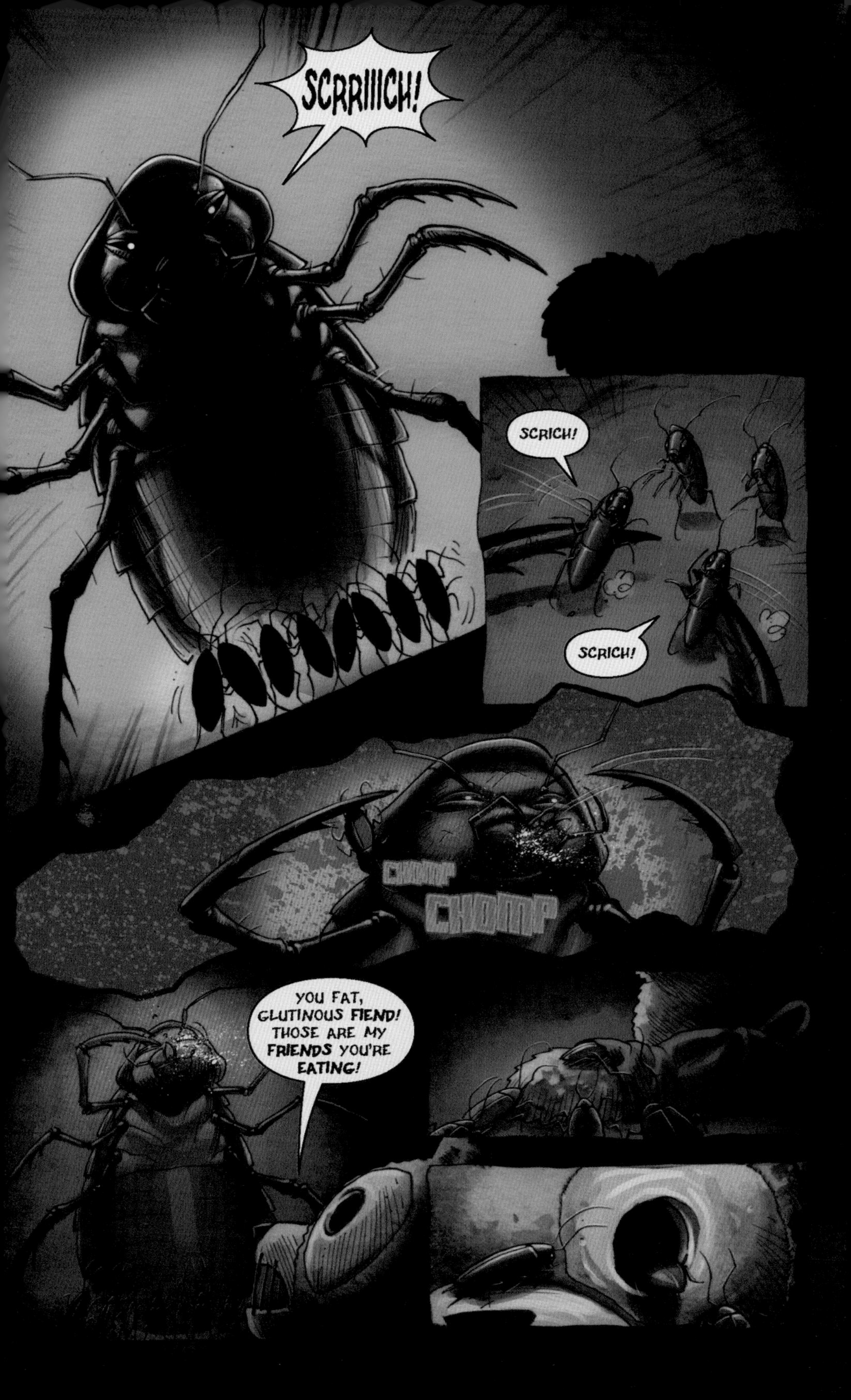
SCRRIIICH!
SCRICH!
SCRICH!
CHOMP
CHOMP
YOU FAT, GLUTINOUS **FIEND!** THOSE ARE MY **FRIENDS** YOU'RE EATING!

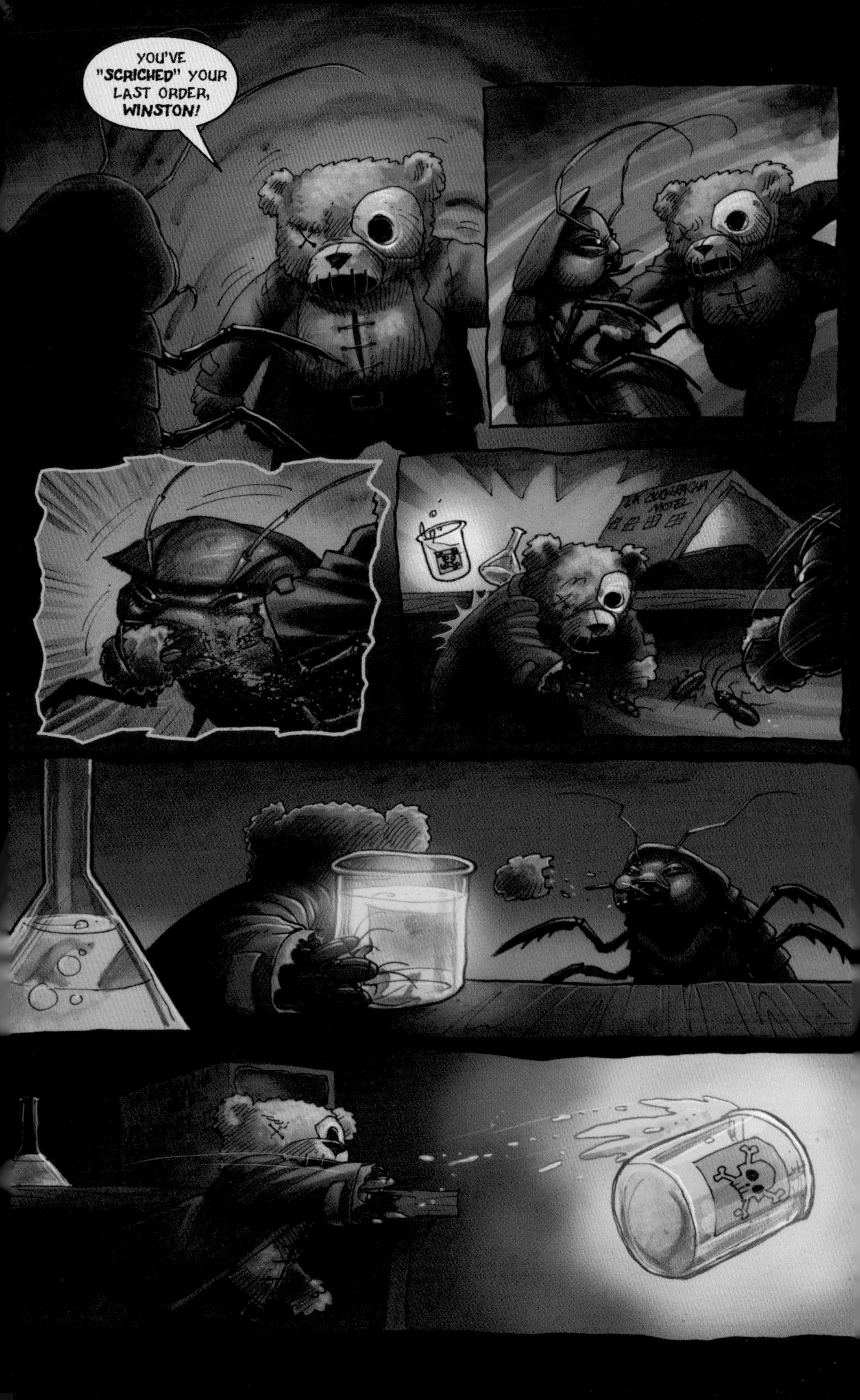
YOU'VE "SCRICHED" YOUR LAST ORDER, WINSTON!
MOTEL

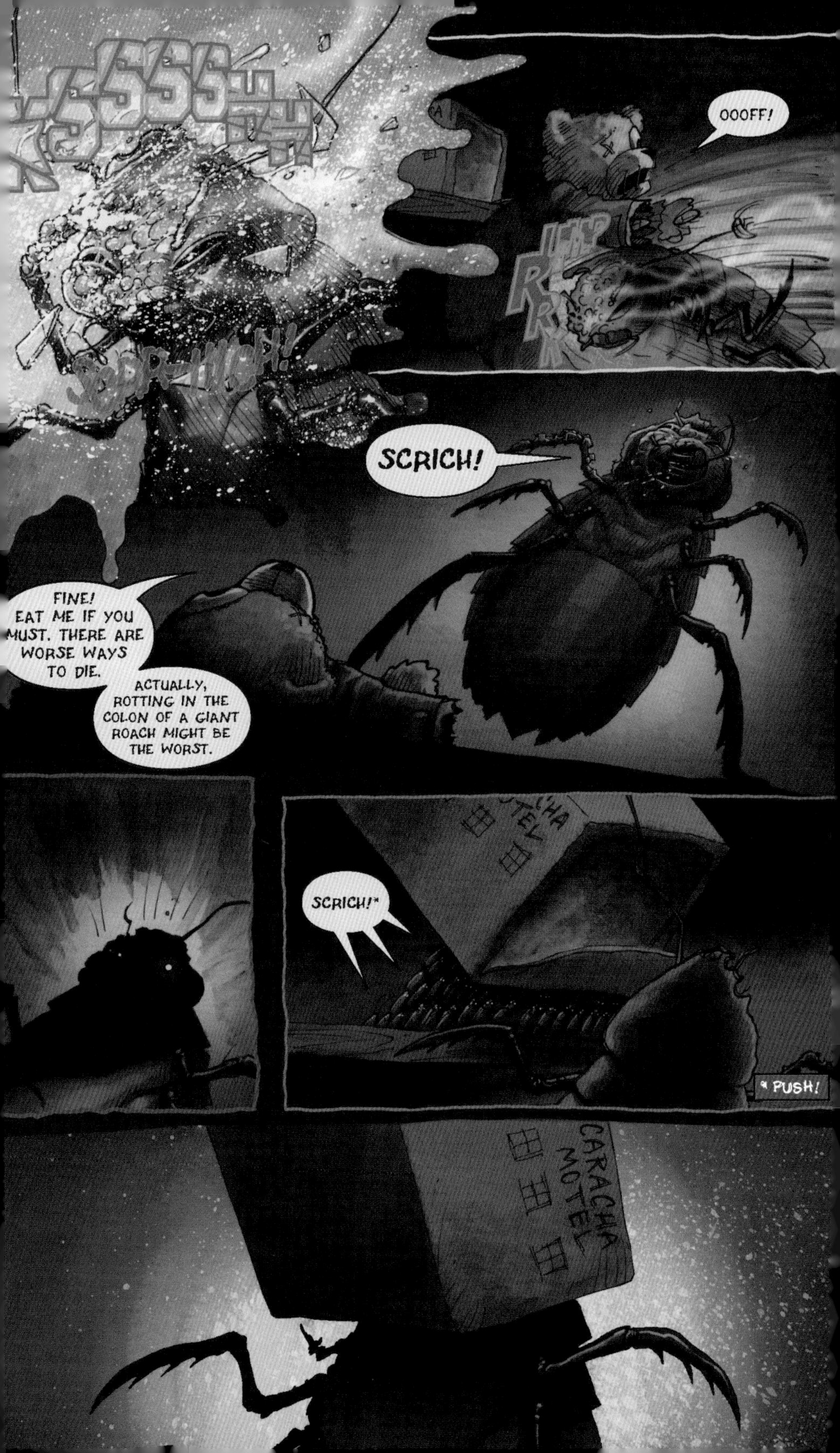

OOOFF!
SCRICH!
FINE! EAT ME IF YOU MUST. THERE ARE WORSE WAYS TO DIE.
ACTUALLY, ROTTING IN THE COLON OF A GIANT ROACH MIGHT BE THE WORST.
SCRICH!*
* PUSH!
CARACHA MOTEL

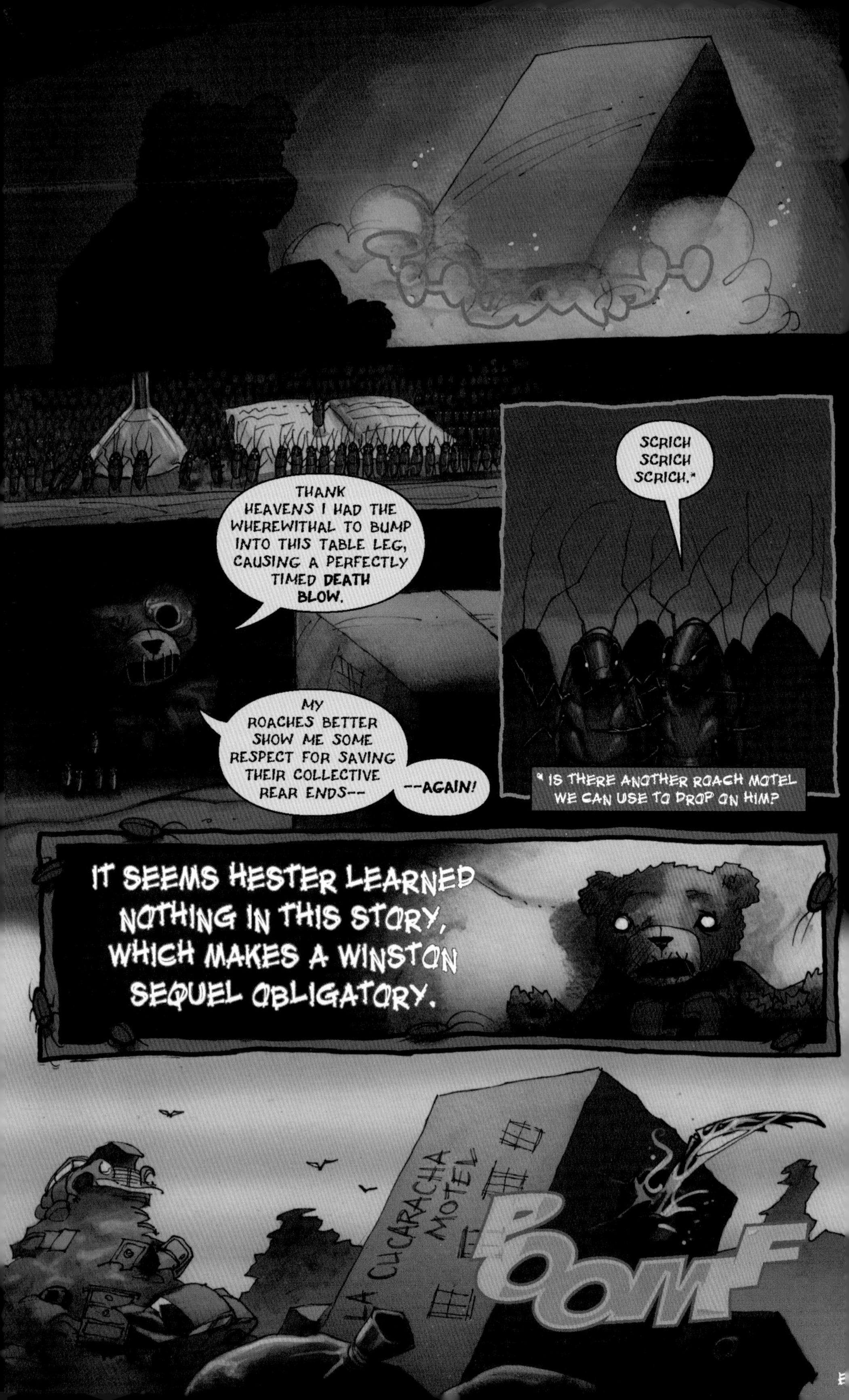
THANK HEAVENS I HAD THE WHEREWITHAL TO BUMP INTO THIS TABLE LEG, CAUSING A PERFECTLY TIMED DEATH BLOW.
MY ROACHES BETTER SHOW ME SOME RESPECT FOR SAVING THEIR COLLECTIVE REAR ENDS--
--AGAIN!
SCRICH SCRICH SCRICH.*
* IS THERE ANOTHER ROACH MOTEL WE CAN USE TO DROP ON HIM?
IT SEEMS HESTER LEARNED NOTHING IN THIS STORY, WHICH MAKES A WINSTON SEQUEL OBLIGATORY.
LA CUCARACHA MOTEL
BOOMF

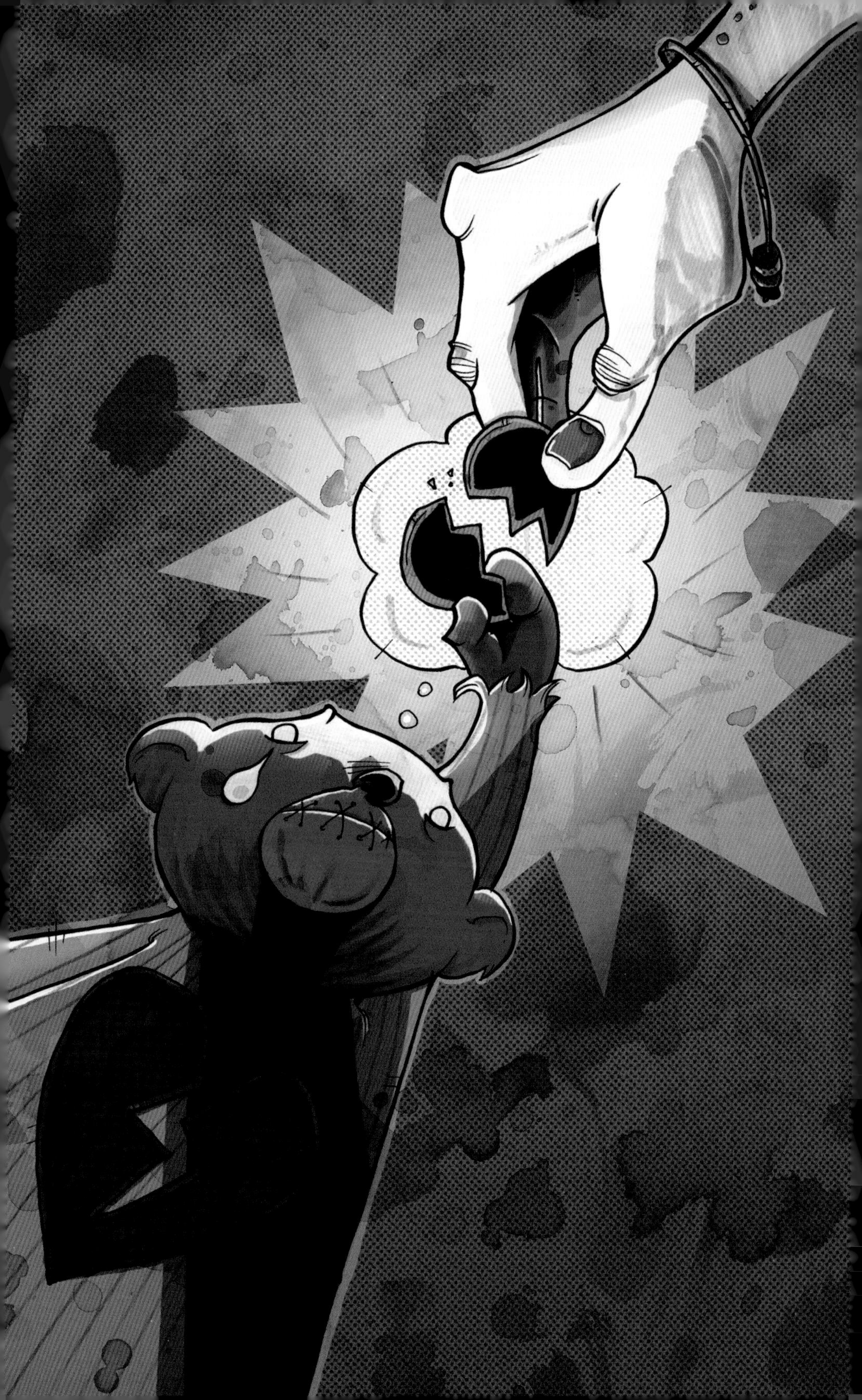

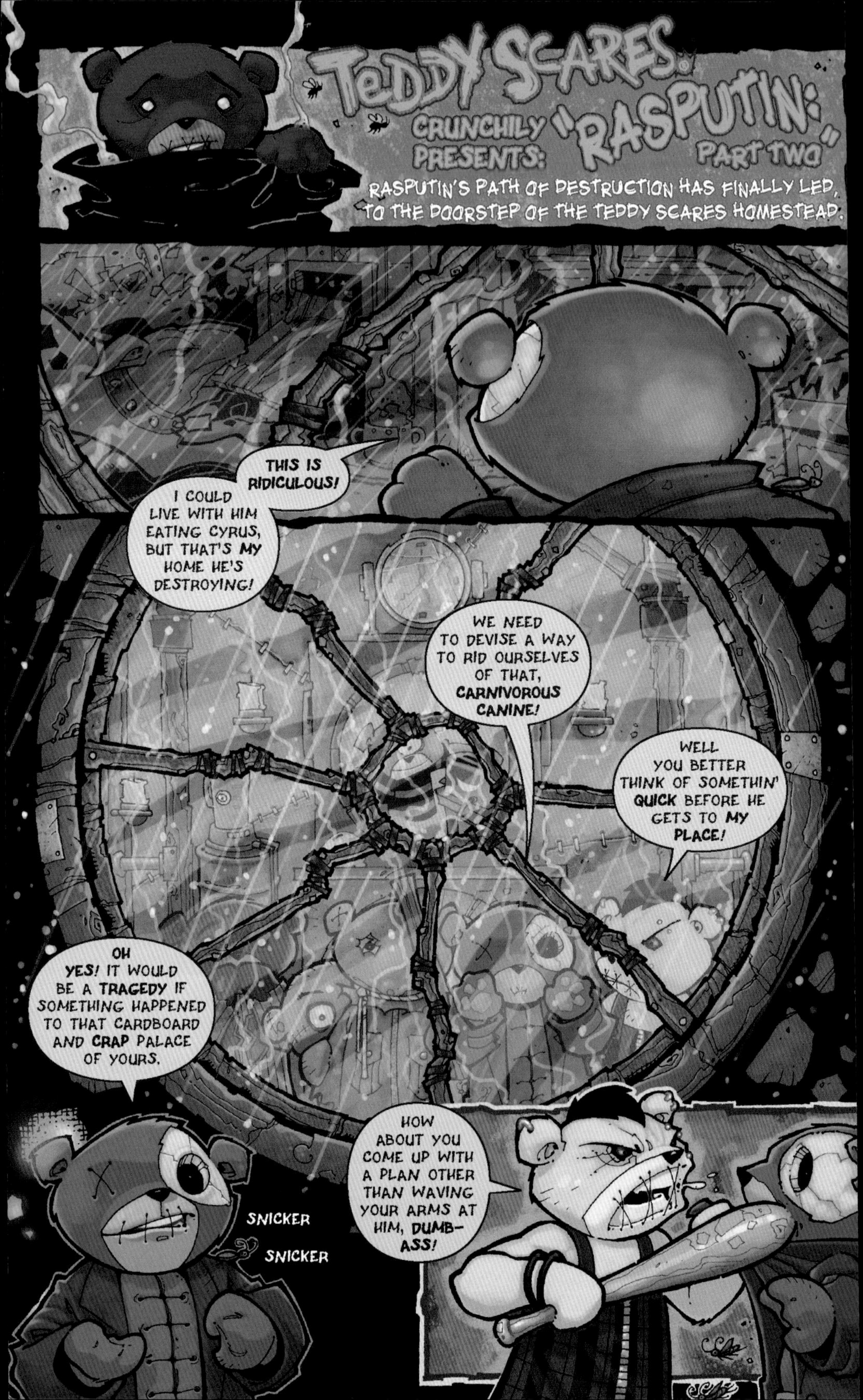
TEDDY SCARES
CRUNCHILY PRESENTS:
"RASPUTIN:" PART TWO
RASPUTIN'S PATH OF DESTRUCTION HAS FINALLY LED, TO THE DOORSTEP OF THE TEDDY SCARES HOMESTEAD.
THIS IS RIDICULOUS!
I COULD LIVE WITH HIM EATING CYRUS, BUT THAT'S MY HOME HE'S DESTROYING!
WE NEED TO DEVISE A WAY TO RID OURSELVES OF THAT, CARNIVOROUS CANINE!
WELL YOU BETTER THINK OF SOMETHIN' QUICK BEFORE HE GETS TO MY PLACE!
OH YES! IT WOULD BE A TRAGEDY IF SOMETHING HAPPENED TO THAT CARDBOARD AND CRAP PALACE OF YOURS.
SNICKER
SNICKER
HOW ABOUT YOU COME UP WITH A PLAN OTHER THAN WAVING YOUR ARMS AT HIM, DUMB-ASS!

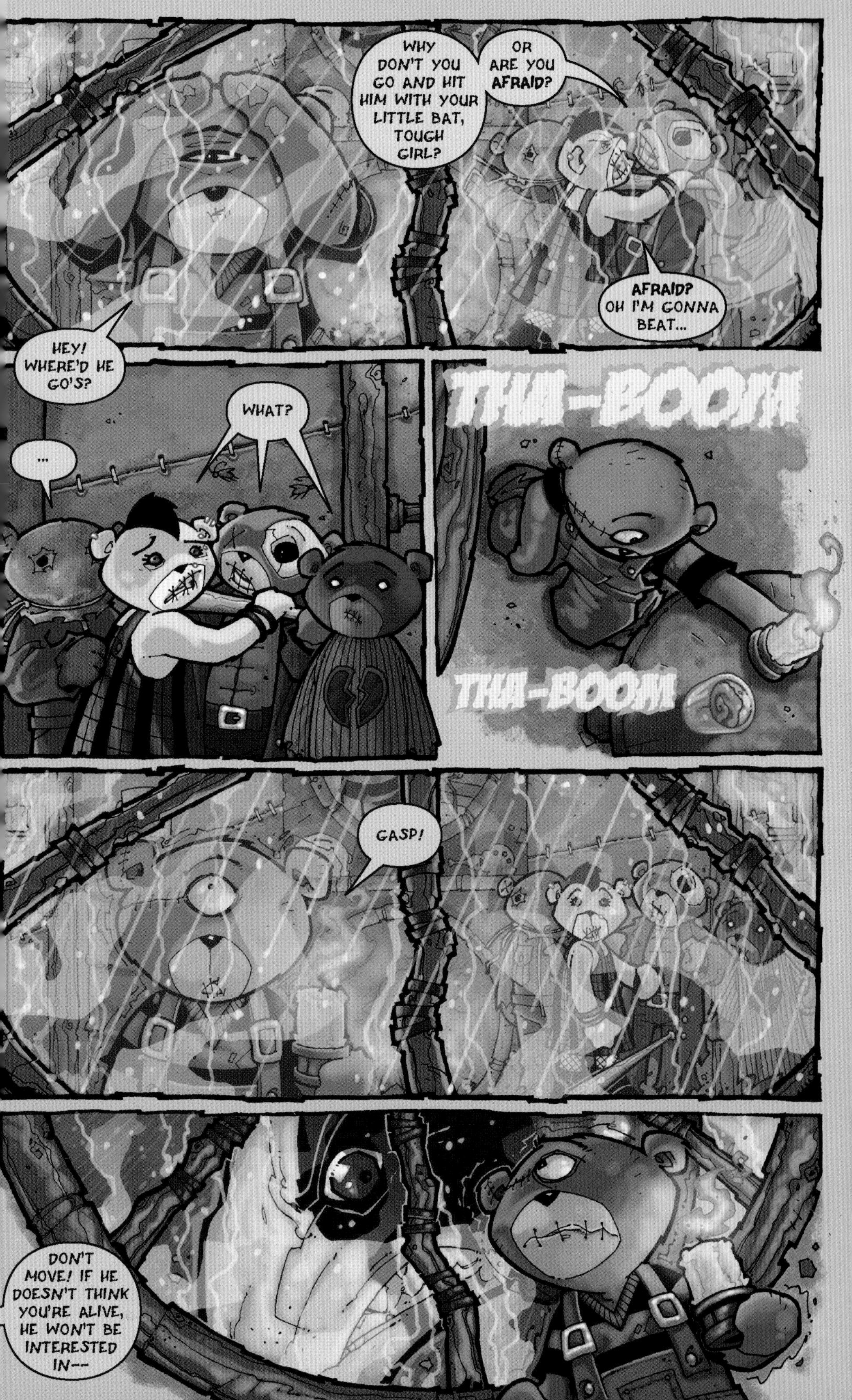
WHY DON'T YOU GO AND HIT HIM WITH YOUR LITTLE BAT, TOUGH GIRL?
OR ARE YOU AFRAID?
AFRAID? OH I'M GONNA BEAT...
HEY! WHERE'D HE GO'S?
WHAT?
...
THA-BOOM
THA-BOOM
GASP!
DON'T MOVE! IF HE DOESN'T THINK YOU'RE ALIVE, HE WON'T BE INTERESTED IN--

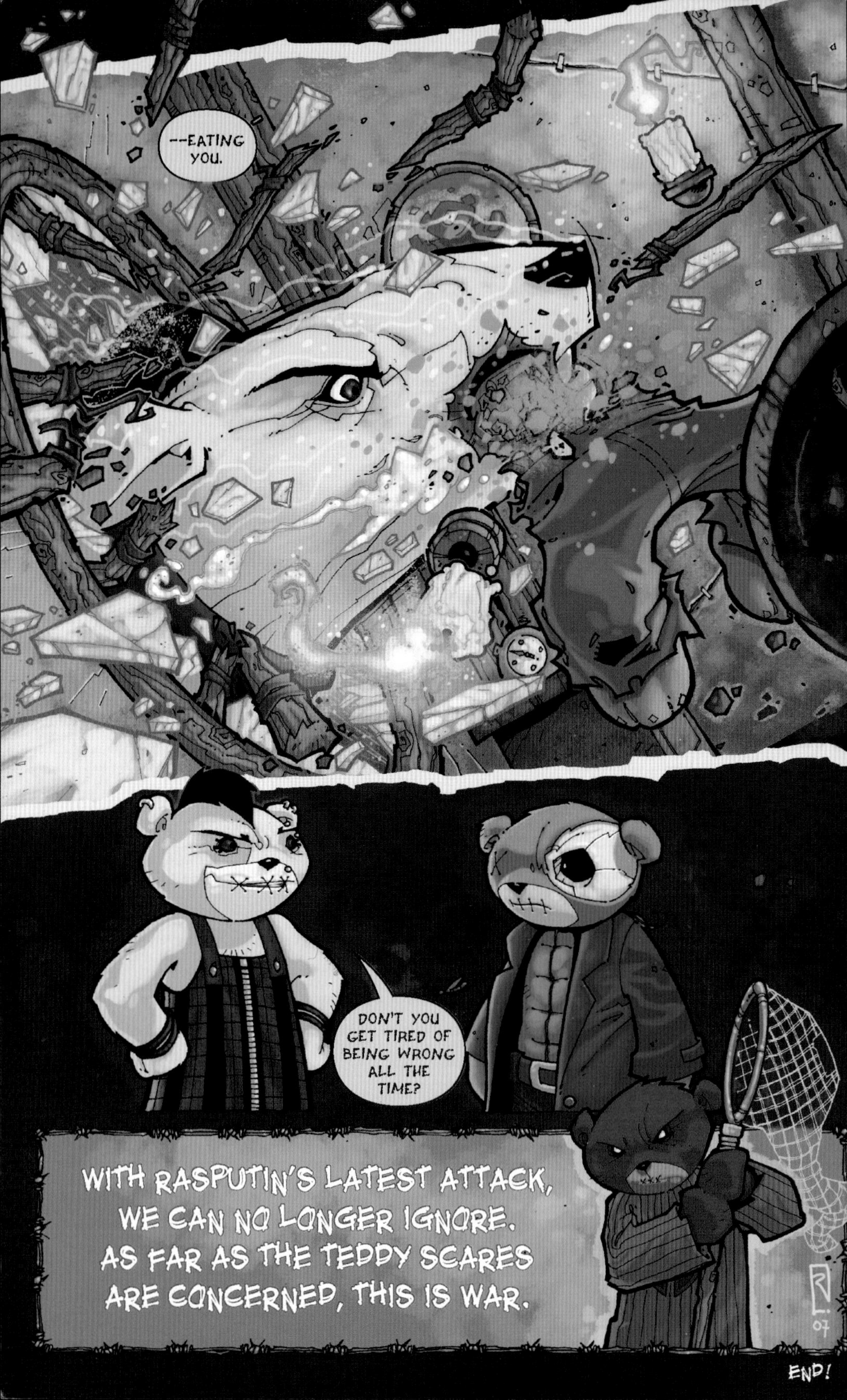
--EATING YOU.
DON'T YOU GET TIRED OF BEING WRONG ALL THE TIME?
WITH RASPUTIN'S LATEST ATTACK, WE CAN NO LONGER IGNORE. AS FAR AS THE TEDDY SCARES ARE CONCERNED, THIS IS WAR.
END!

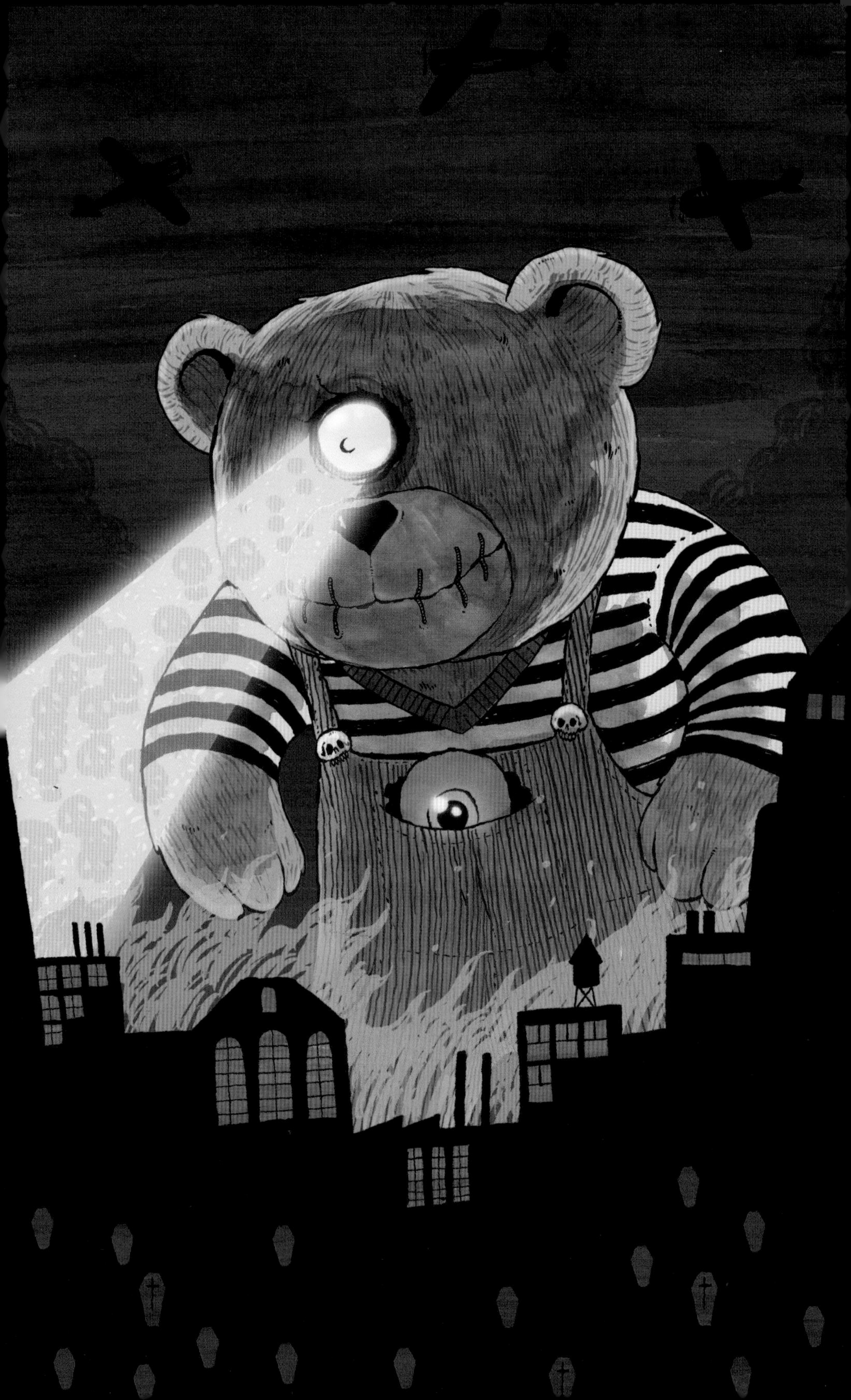

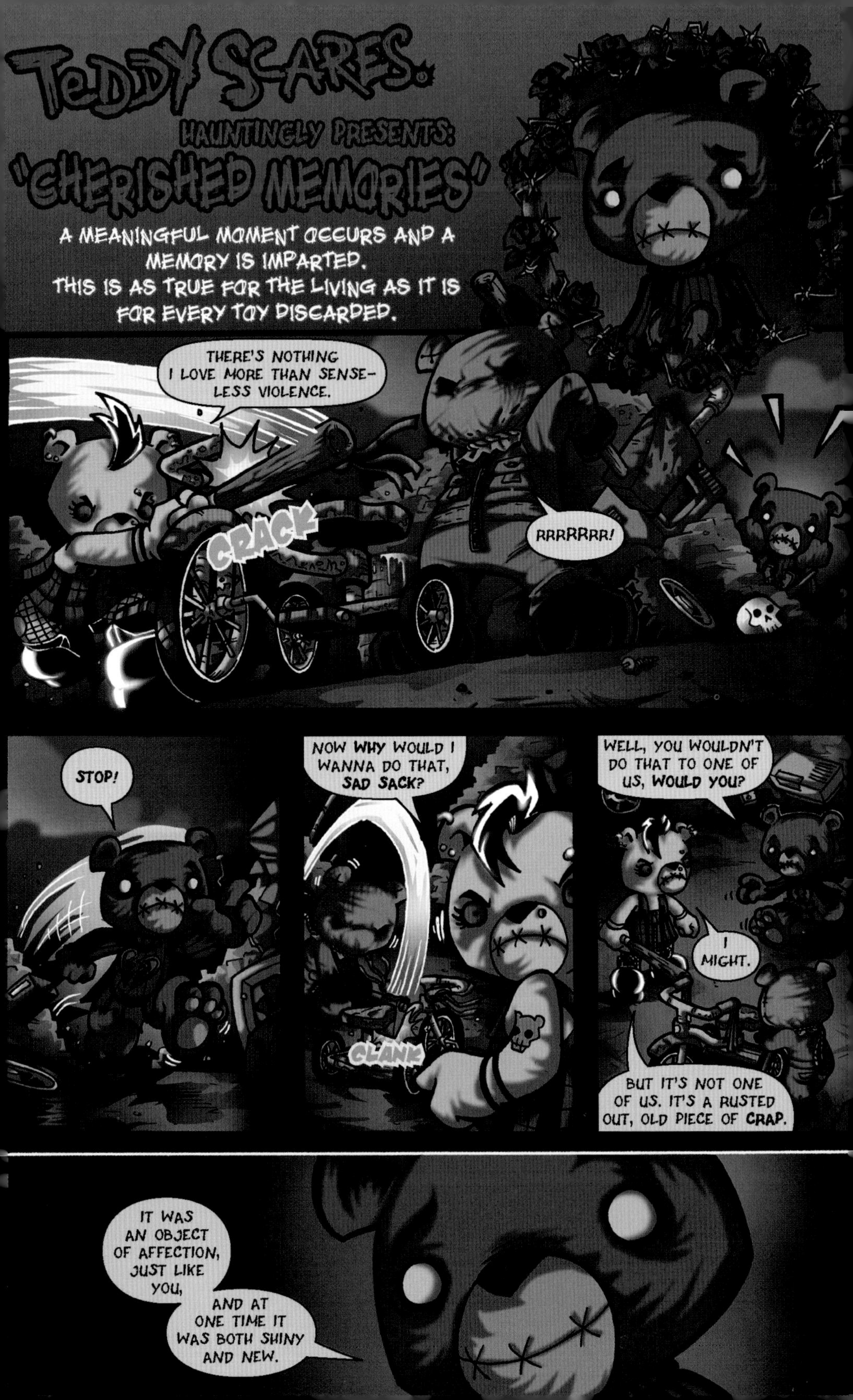
TEDDY SCARES.
HAUNTINGLY PRESENTS:
"CHERISHED MEMORIES"
A MEANINGFUL MOMENT OCCURS AND A MEMORY IS IMPARTED.
THIS IS AS TRUE FOR THE LIVING AS IT IS FOR EVERY TOY DISCARDED.
THERE'S NOTHING I LOVE MORE THAN SENSE-LESS VIOLENCE.
CRACK
RRRRRRR!
STOP!
NOW WHY WOULD I WANNA DO THAT, SAD SACK?
CLANK
WELL, YOU WOULDN'T DO THAT TO ONE OF US, WOULD YOU?
I MIGHT.
BUT IT'S NOT ONE OF US. IT'S A RUSTED OUT, OLD PIECE OF CRAP.
IT WAS AN OBJECT OF AFFECTION, JUST LIKE YOU,
AND AT ONE TIME IT WAS BOTH SHINY AND NEW.

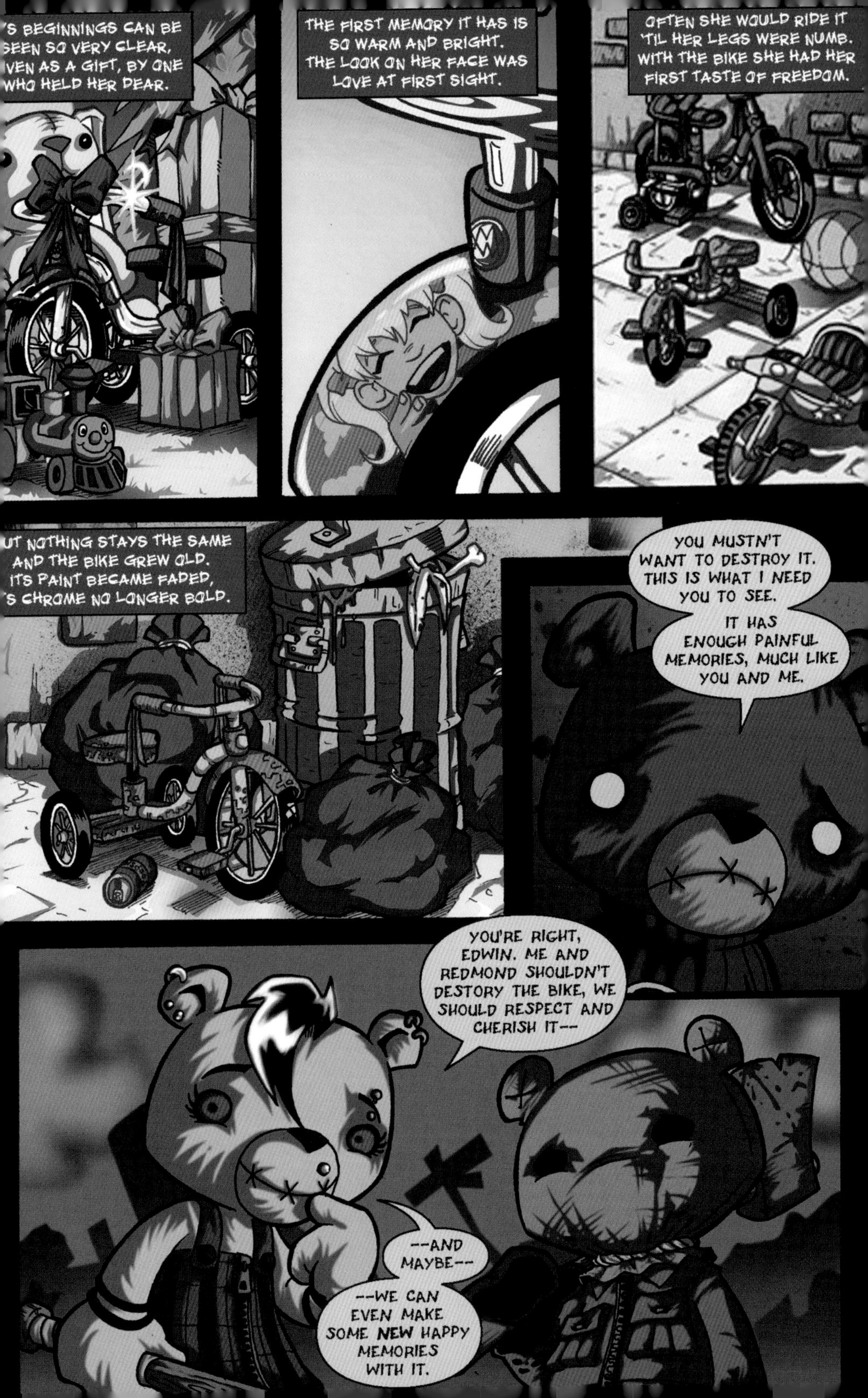
'S BEGINNINGS CAN BE SEEN SO VERY CLEAR, IVEN AS A GIFT, BY ONE WHO HELD HER DEAR.
THE FIRST MEMORY IT HAS IS SO WARM AND BRIGHT. THE LOOK ON HER FACE WAS LOVE AT FIRST SIGHT.
OFTEN SHE WOULD RIDE IT 'TIL HER LEGS WERE NUMB. WITH THE BIKE SHE HAD HER FIRST TASTE OF FREEDOM.
UT NOTHING STAYS THE SAME AND THE BIKE GREW OLD. ITS PAINT BECAME FADED, 'S CHROME NO LONGER BOLD.
YOU MUSTN'T WANT TO DESTROY IT. THIS IS WHAT I NEED YOU TO SEE.
IT HAS ENOUGH PAINFUL MEMORIES, MUCH LIKE YOU AND ME.
YOU'RE RIGHT, EDWIN. ME AND REDMOND SHOULDN'T DESTORY THE BIKE, WE SHOULD RESPECT AND CHERISH IT--
--AND MAYBE--
--WE CAN EVEN MAKE SOME NEW HAPPY MEMORIES WITH IT.

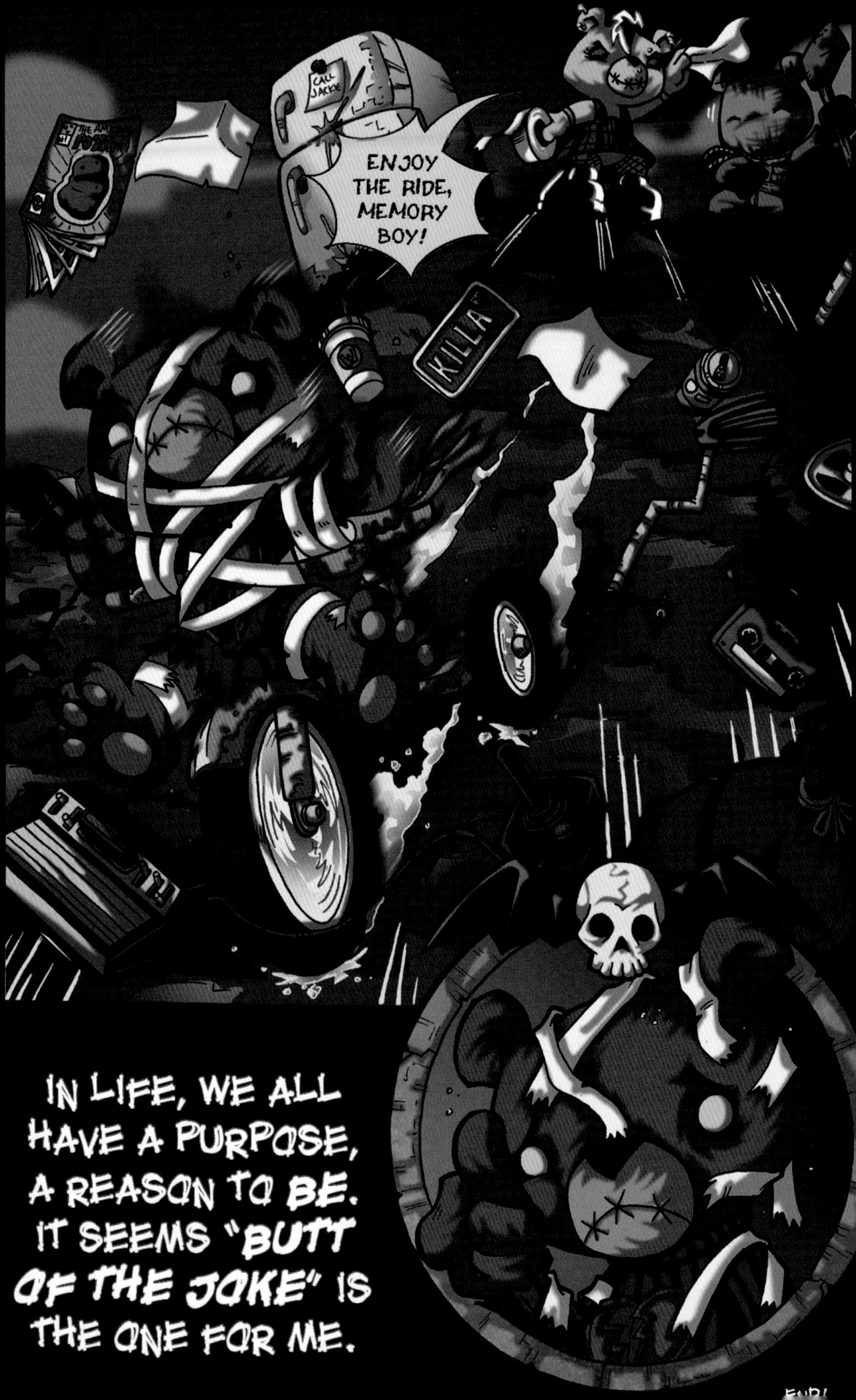
CALL JACKIE
ENJOY THE RIDE, MEMORY BOY!
KILLA
IN LIFE, WE ALL HAVE A PURPOSE, A REASON TO BE. IT SEEMS "BUTT OF THE JOKE" IS THE ONE FOR ME.

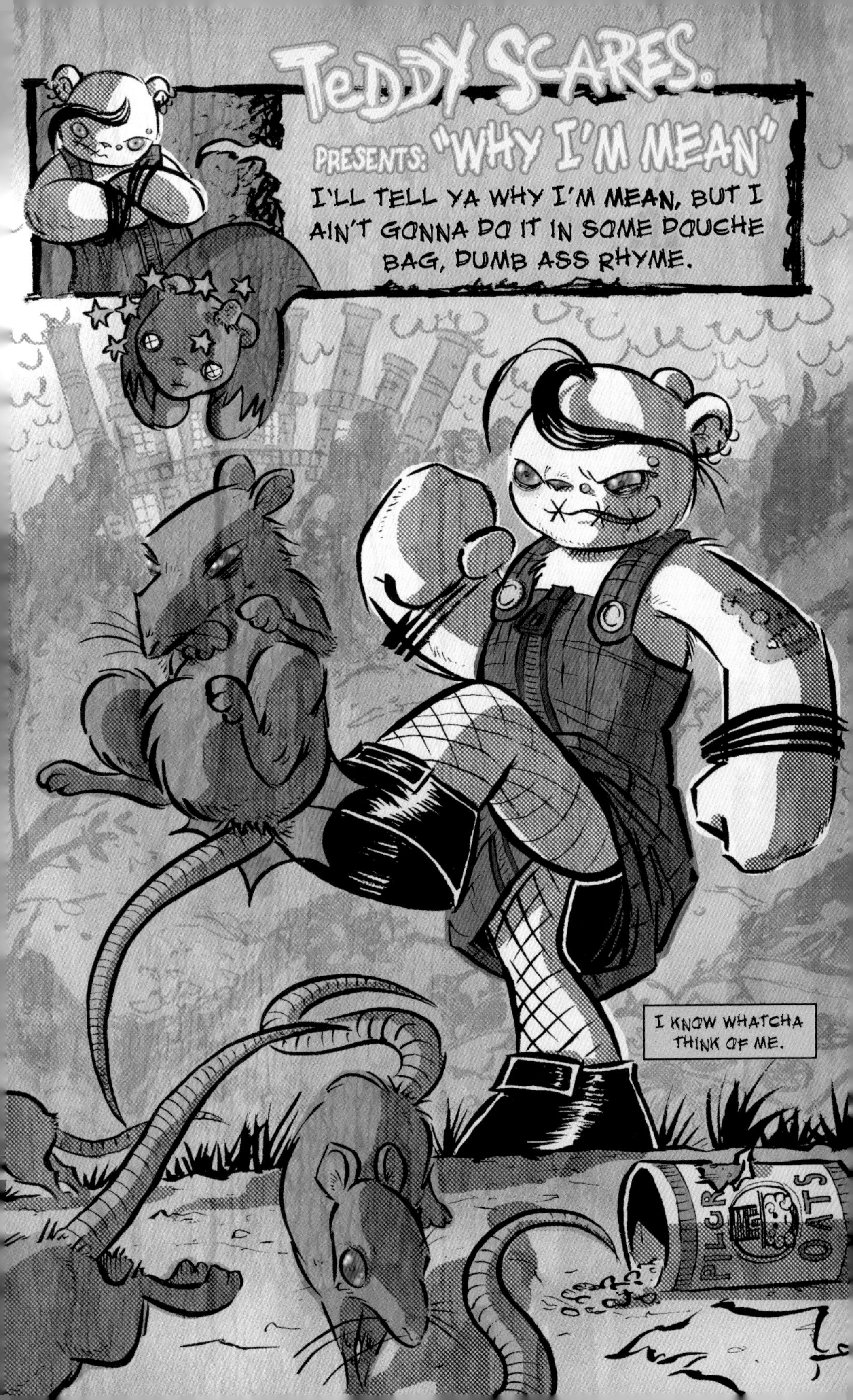
TEDDY SCARES.
PRESENTS: "WHY I'M MEAN"
I'LL TELL YA WHY I'M MEAN, BUT I AIN'T GONNA DO IT IN SOME DOUCHE BAG, DUMB ASS RHYME.
I KNOW WHATCHA THINK OF ME.
PILGRIM OATS

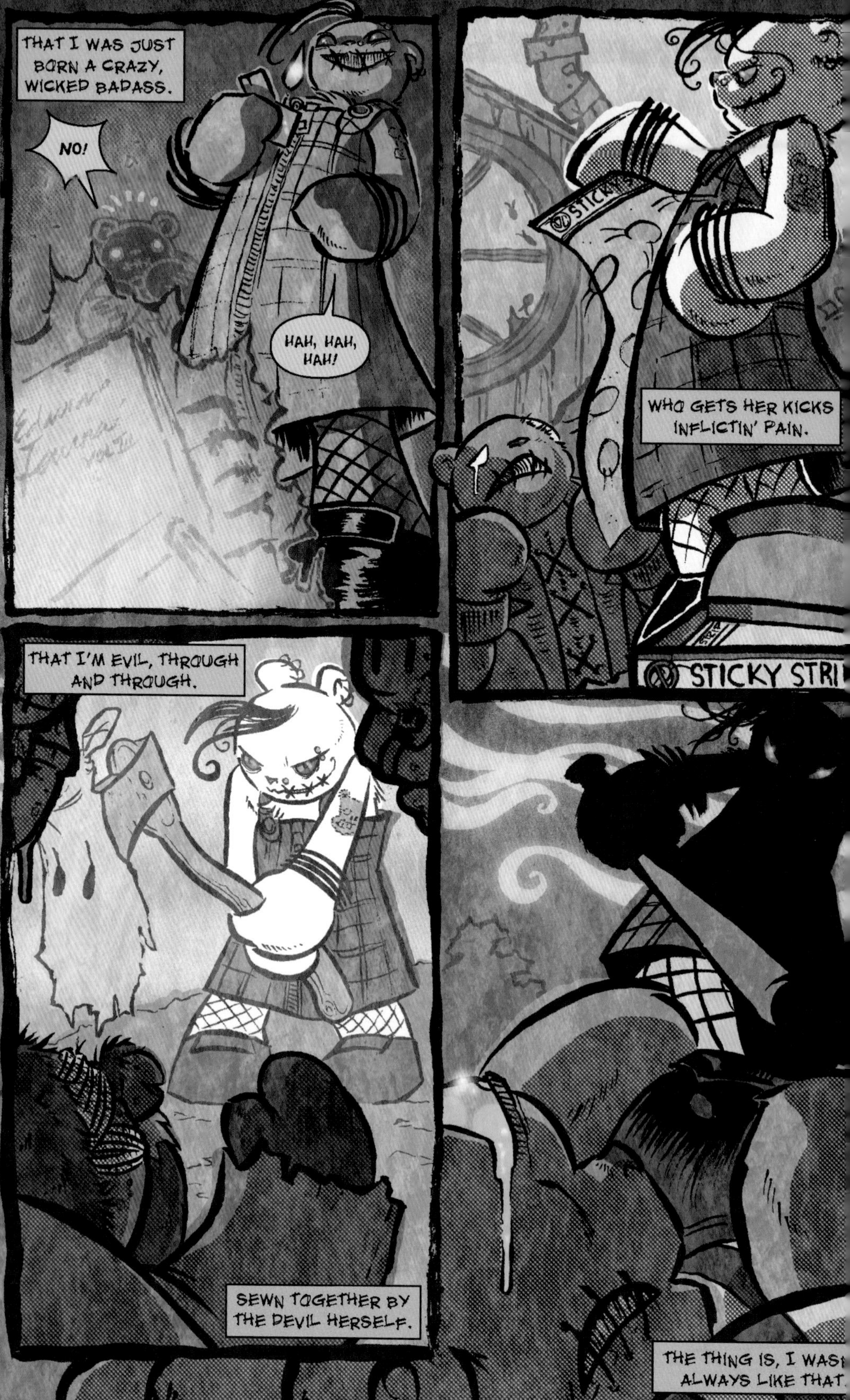
THAT I WAS JUST BORN A CRAZY, WICKED BADASS.
NO!
HAH, HAH, HAH!
WHO GETS HER KICKS INFLICTIN' PAIN.
STICKY STRI
THAT I'M EVIL, THROUGH AND THROUGH.
SEWN TOGETHER BY THE DEVIL HERSELF.
THE THING IS, I WAS
ALWAYS LIKE THAT.

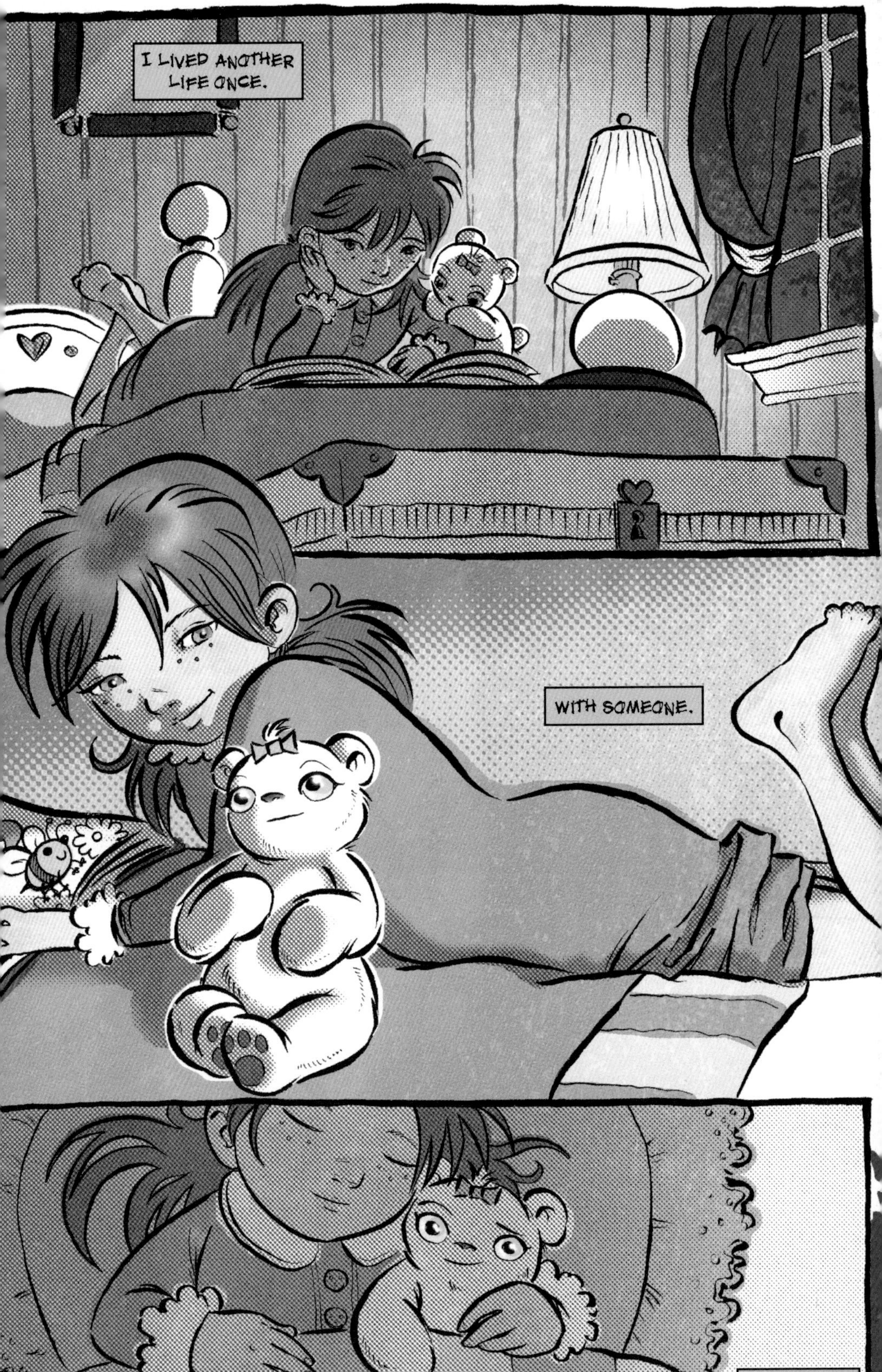
I LIVED ANOTHER LIFE ONCE.
WITH SOMEONE.
NOT ALONE.

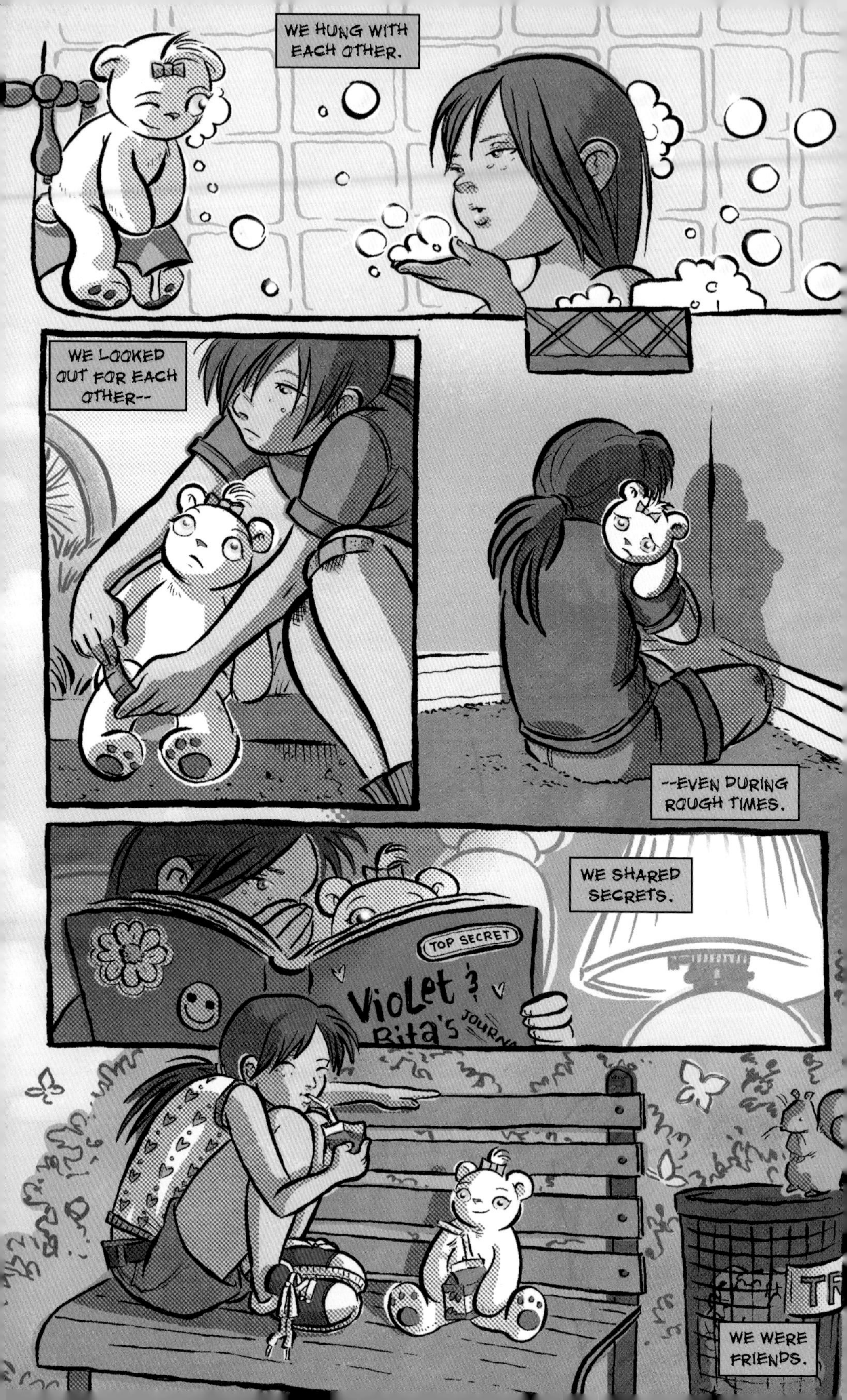
WE HUNG WITH EACH OTHER.
WE LOOKED OUT FOR EACH OTHER--
--EVEN DURING ROUGH TIMES.
WE SHARED SECRETS.
TOP SECRET
Violet
Rita's
WE WERE FRIENDS.

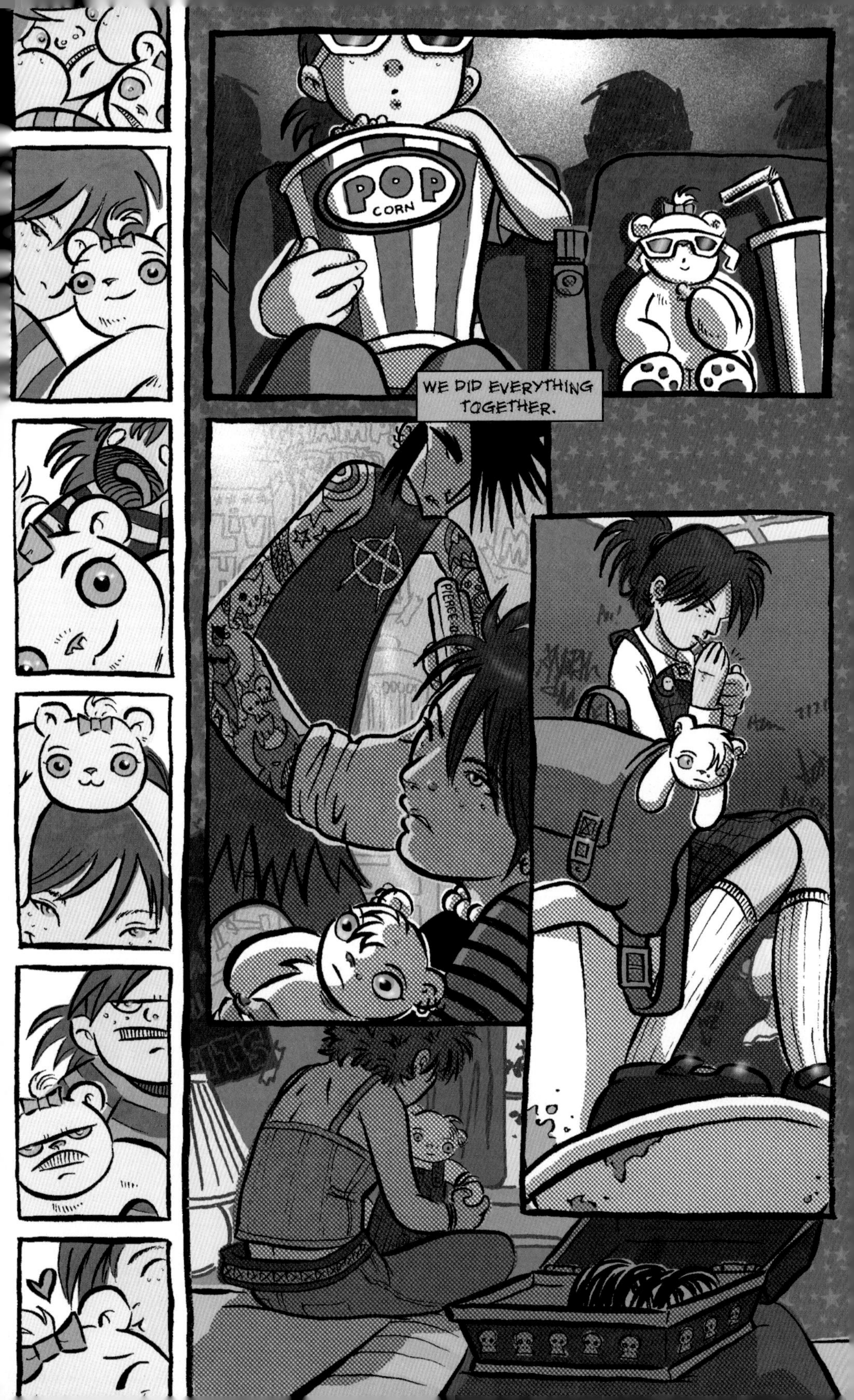
WE DID EVERYTHING TOGETHER.
POP CORN

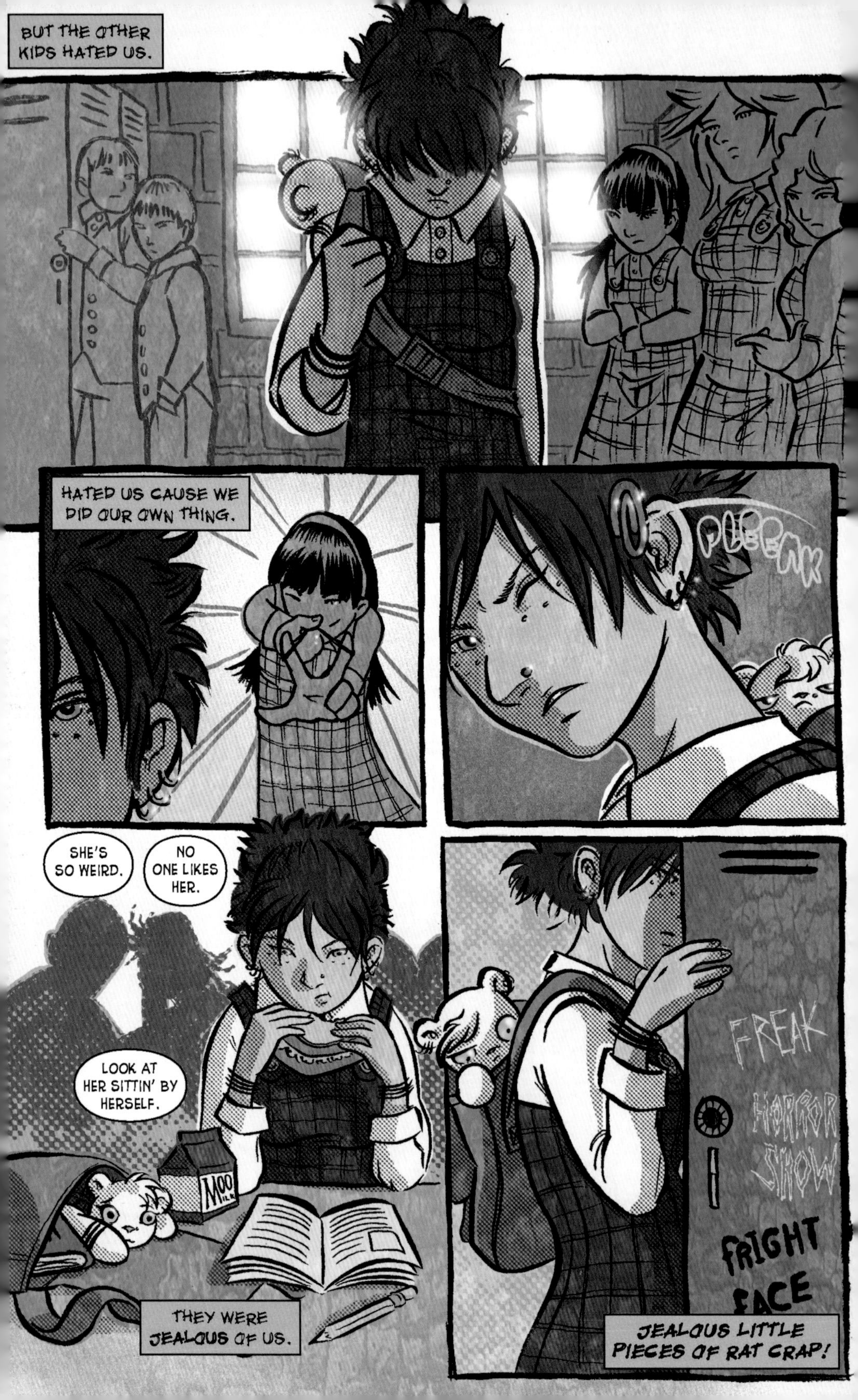
BUT THE OTHER KIDS HATED US.
HATED US CAUSE WE DID OUR OWN THING.
PLEEMK
SHE'S SO WEIRD.
NO ONE LIKES HER.
LOOK AT HER SITTIN' BY HERSELF.
MOO
THEY WERE JEALOUS OF US.
FREAK
HORROR SHOW
FRIGHT FACE
JEALOUS LITTLE PIECES OF RAT CRAP!

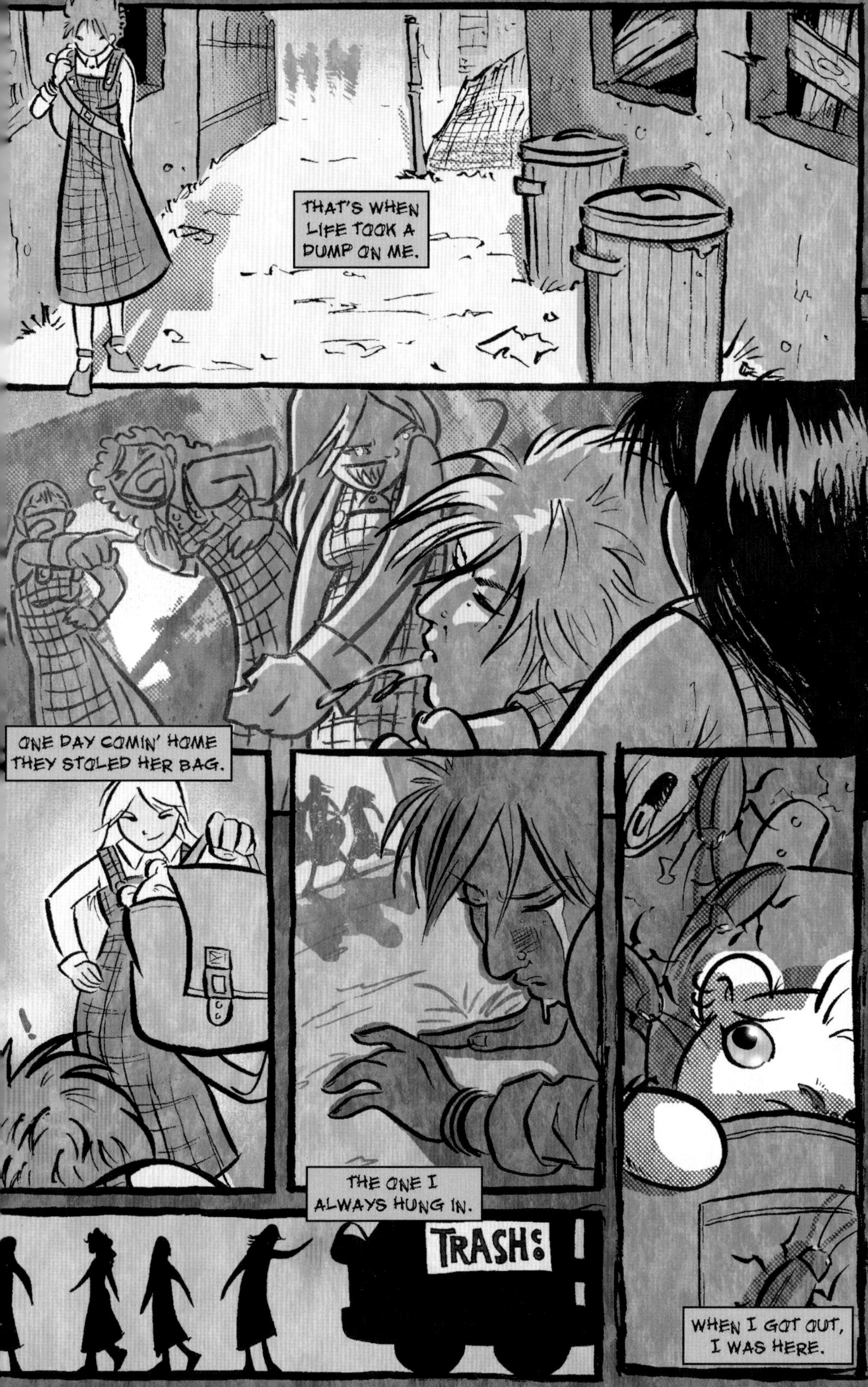
THAT'S WHEN LIFE TOOK A DUMP ON ME.
ONE DAY COMIN' HOME THEY STOLED HER BAG.
THE ONE I ALWAYS HUNG IN.
TRASH CO
WHEN I GOT OUT, I WAS HERE.

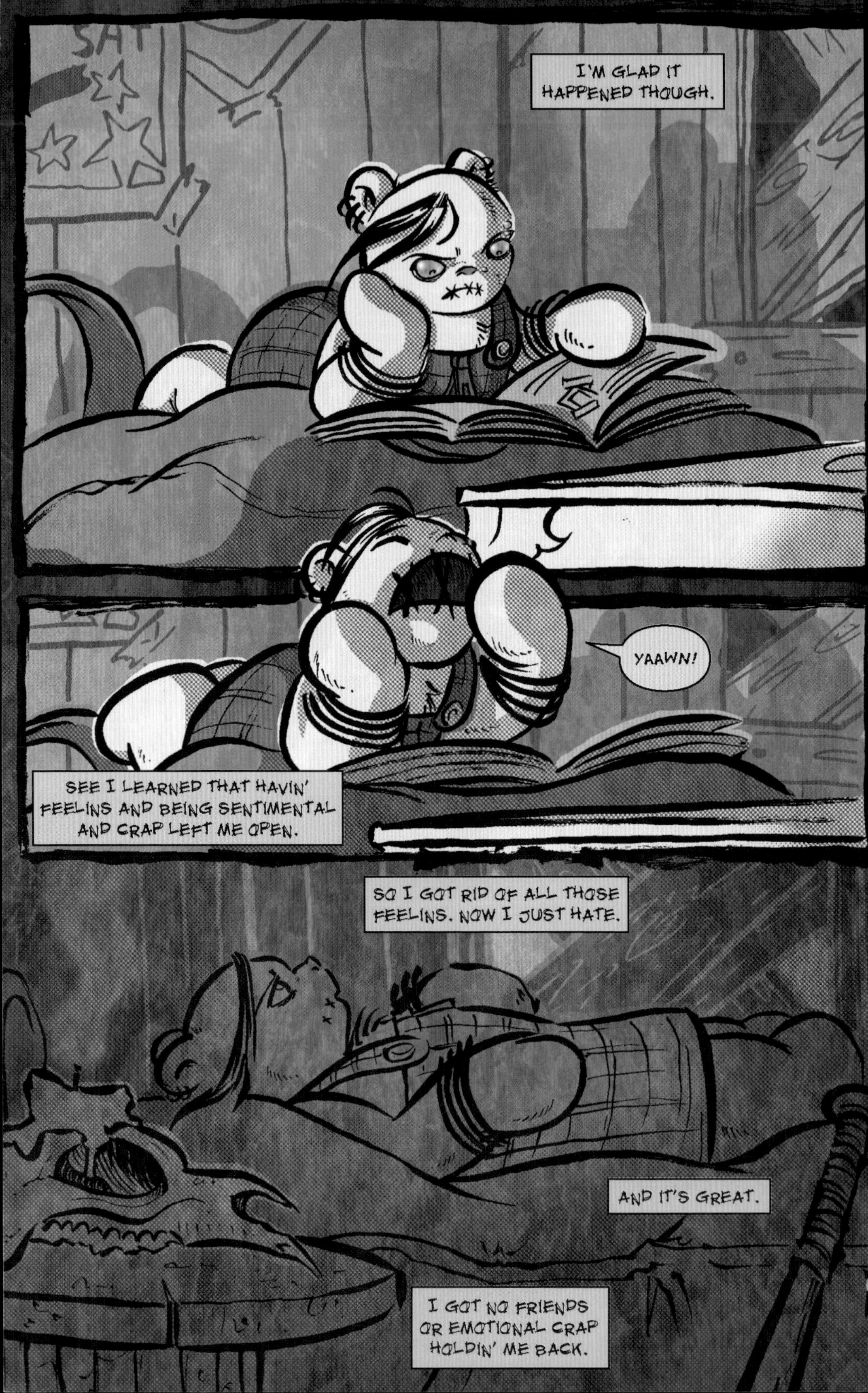

I'M GLAD IT HAPPENED THOUGH.
YAAWN!
SEE I LEARNED THAT HAVIN' FEELINS AND BEING SENTIMENTAL AND CRAP LEFT ME OPEN.
SO I GOT RID OF ALL THOSE FEELINS. NOW I JUST HATE.
AND IT'S GREAT.
I GOT NO FRIENDS OR EMOTIONAL CRAP HOLDIN' ME BACK.

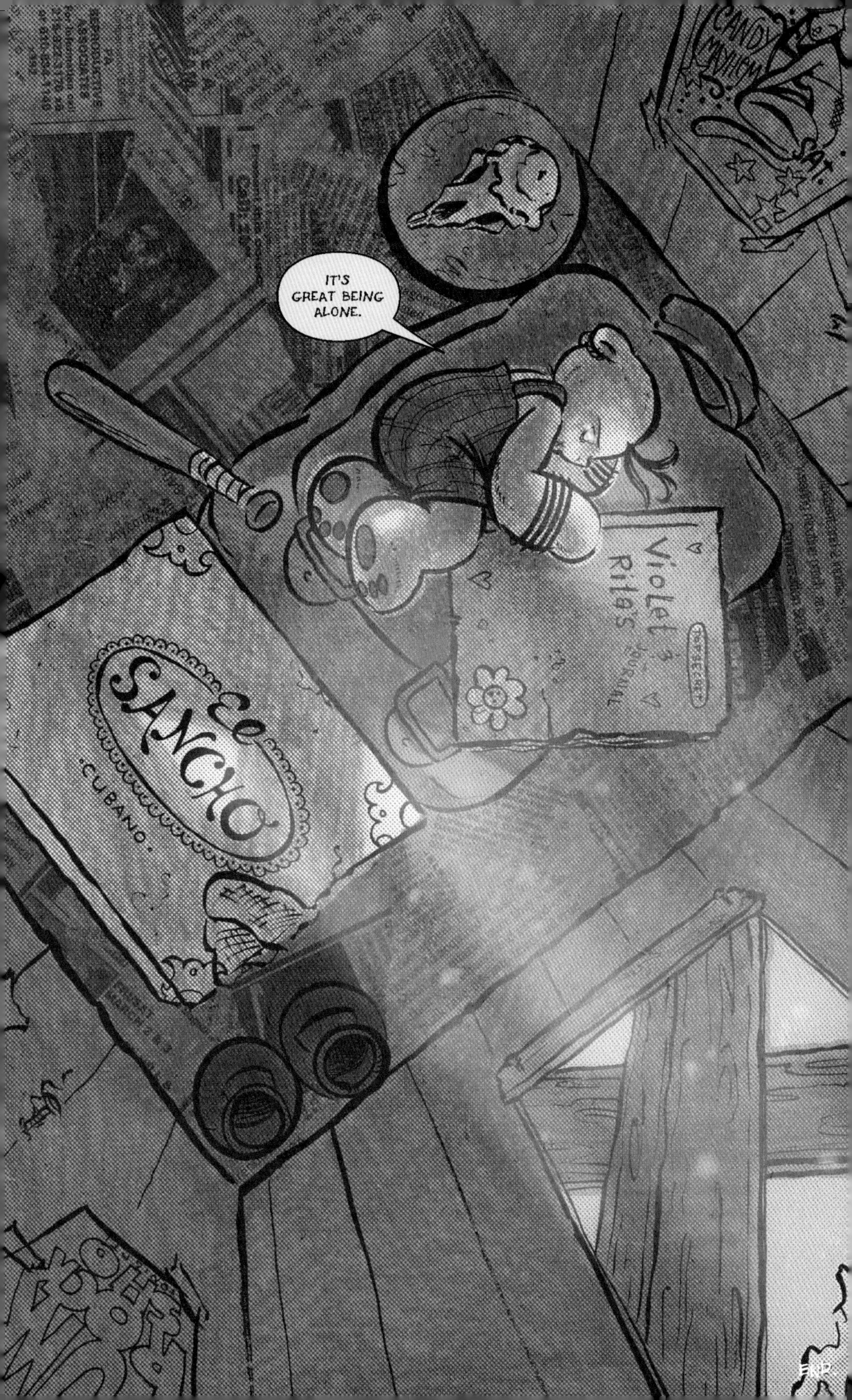
IT'S GREAT BEING ALONE.
EL SANCHO
CUBANO
END

Mundy Drudge™

Sheldon Grogg™

Mazey Podge™

Granger Evermore™

Eli Wretch™

TEDDY SCARES®

ONCE SOFT AND CUDDLY
NOW DEAD AND BLOODY

Admit it. You lusted for them. You displayed them.
You slept with them every night. And then, one day,
you dumped your teddy bear. They used to be cuddly and
cute. But no more. Maybe it's vengeance that turns teddy
bears into Teddy Scares. Nevertheless, they're back from
the dead, and they're pissed.

Each adorable aberration is 12" tall, irresistibly plush
and grossly attired in real fabric clothing and eerie
accessories. Fresh from the morgue, they arrive complete
with a toe tag, entombed in a window-display box.

Lock your doors, board up your windows and log on to:

www.TeddyScares.com

Also available in 6"
MORGUE MINIS™

Rita
Mortis